Luna: Puppy D...

No-Slack Jack

No-Slack Jack

Book #2

Written and Illustrated by Kesmine G. Hickman

ISBN: 1480087971
ISBN-13: 978-1480087972
Library of Congress Control Number: 2012919292
CreateSpace Independent Publishing Platform
North Charleston, South Carolina

To: Reese

Luna's back!

Kesmine
Hickman
11/9/13

*Dedicated to my snooty
Shih Tzu, Luna, and her
adorable daughter, Leia*

The *Luna: Puppy Detective* series:

Luna: Puppy Detective #1: Catnapped!

Luna: Puppy Detective #2: No-Slack Jack

Also by Kesmine Hickman:

Kathy Carts: Mystery Series

Important Notation by Me—Luna

Dear Reader,

I am about to tell you the story of my second mysterious case, "No-Slack Jack." If you haven't read my first case, "Catnapped!" that's okay. This mystery is entirely different.

Who am I? Well, that's an easy one—I'm Luna, Puppy Detective, queen of the Hickman household and world-famous Shih Tzu (pronounced "Sheet Zoo") sleuth! In short, I'm awesome. Keep that in mind as I tell the story, little Luna kid fans.

Okay, so before we get started with the roller coaster of clues, suspects, and displays of awesomeness from yours truly, I want to introduce a few things. First, there's Sierra Vista, Arizona, the town where I reside. In a word, it's hot. There we go. Sierra Vista has been introduced. The next thing on my imaginary list is my house. It's a big two-story stucco structure, and inside, in the living room, is my wondrous Snuggy Rug. Occupying this house besides me are the humans—Emily, who is twelve years old, and Mr. and Mrs. Hickman, who are Emily's parents (I don't know how old they are). Then there are the animals—Leia Jewel, my daughter, who is charcoal gray, chubby, peppy, clueless, and lazy, all rolled up into one like a gigantic Shih Tzu burrito. Creeper is next—he's a little gray kitten that I've taken under my paw. The only reason I'm raising him, mind you, is that he's not a typical cat. He says "please" and "thank you" and doesn't scratch curtains or chase mice or twitch his tail or any of those annoying cat things that cats do. I'm proud to note that he even barks like a dog! Ah, I'm such a good parent.

Anyway, on to the irritating residents of the Hickman house—the cats, Lily and Monikk. Lily is a black, white, and brown, short-haired, sneaky little nuisance, with a pink twitching nose and a mischievous attitude. Monikk is her right-paw cat, who steals (and shreds) my beautiful squeakies when I'm not around. Long-haired and prissy, which is typical of all Persians, Monikk thinks she's princess of the house, with Lily being queen. But the truth is, I rule, and they're not even my subjects. They're more like... like...like the janitors the queen hires to mop up the urine when Leia makes an uh-oh (though they often neglect their duties).

In the yard behind mine, there lives yet another feline foe (alliteration—"f" words!) of mine, Pip the Siamese. For those of you out there who are thinking that Pip is a cute name, this cat is far from cute or loveable. But what can I expect? She's a cat.

This mystery is about my mishap that occurred because of said Pip the Siamese. Let's just put it this way: She's not only annoying, she's also conniving. She *will stop at nothing to humiliate me. However, in this particular case, I actually ended up discovering the case of No-Slack Jack because of Pip. Do I give her credit for that? Of course not. I discovered the case all on my own. I deserve all the kudos, and I especially deserve praise for nabbing... Wait, that would give it all away, huh? Enjoy.*

Luna, Puppy Detective

CHAPTER ONE (I, *Uno*)

Canine Checkers Goes Awry

"It's your move, Mommy," Leia told me, wagging her tubby tail ("t" words!) as she sat by my Snuggy Rug.

I studied the piece of kibble, which was almost halfway along the length of the Snuggy Rug. *Hmmm. What should I do?* I had already collected four total Rights. That meant I could move four different ways. But they all had to be *different.*

Okay, let me just explain this game to you before we go on. It's called Canine Checkers. It's like a combination of human charades and human checkers, with a bit of canine rules thrown in. First, each player gets a piece of kibble and sets it on one side of the Snuggy Rug. Then one player acts something out, and the remaining two players try to guess what that player is doing. Whoever guesses correctly gets what's called a Right, which means he or she can either move immediately or wait until they have several Rights. A Right is basically the ability to move your kibble in a certain pattern—a zigzag, a straight line, a jump, etc. Every time a player uses a Right, it has to be a different pattern. For example, if I made my kibble zigzag on one turn, I wouldn't be able to zigzag again for the entire game. The purpose of Rights is for maneuvering and advancing—but you can only use one Right to cover distances of one to two Dewclaws, which are equivalent to one to two inches. The object is to eventually get to the end of the Snuggy Rug. Whoever gets to the end of the Snuggy Rug first wins the game—and also all the kibble pieces (yum!). Players aren't allowed to remind other players what Rights they've already used, and if you use a Right (like a zigzag) more than once, you're automatically disqualified.

At that moment, I had four Rights. The board didn't look that great for me. Creeper was a couple Dewclaws ahead of me, and Leia wasn't far behind him. Grimacing, I balanced my kibble piece on my paw, moving it two Dewclaws in a zigzag fashion, over Creeper's kibble, and then in a forward fashion, toward the end of the Snuggy Rug, for one Dewclaw. I used my next Right to move sideways in front of Leia's kibble (so she'd have to jump over me if she wanted to reach the end), and then I did a hop Right and ended up significantly closer to the Snuggy Rug's edge.

Ha. I'm so awesome.

"Now you have to do a charade," Leia chirped, grinning from ear to chubby ear. "Be a penguin," she recommended. "I know how to guess that."

"Leia, I'm not going to be a *penguin* just because you want me to be," I spat in annoyance. I stood on my hind legs and began hopping up and down, spinning in repeated circles. "Now," I challenged as I continued my routine, "what am I?"

"A penguin!" Leia burst out instantly.

I just told her…! Ugh, never mind.

"*No,*" I growled, spinning in another circle. My hind leg muscles were beginning to hurt from the strain of holding myself up for so long, and my vision blurred with dizziness. Couldn't Leia and Creeper hurry up and guess?

Speaking of Creeper, my gray-haired, green-eyed cat son had one paw to his chin, obviously deep in thought. He was tracing my movements carefully, his tail ramrod straight, without even the tip curled over. Creeper wished he could be a dog, and his stance made his longing apparent as he opened his mouth to pant.

"A black-and-white, flightless species indigenous to areas near the Antarctic Circle!" Leia tried again.

I squinted, still spinning. "*What?*"

"A penguin," Leia simplified.

I rolled my eyes. "Leia, I am *not* a penguin."

"Of course not, Mommy." Leia beamed, as if she were talking to a pawddler. She giggled quite childishly. "You're a *dog.* To be specific, you're a female Shih Tzu, black and white, with a pale moon shape on your head, hence your name, *Luna,* which is the Spanish word for *moon,* which is a word in Spanish, and Spanish people are the people in Mexico and Spain, and that's why it's *Spanish,* Mommy, though I don't know why it's called that and not *Spain*ish, since it's *Spain,* not *Span,* but maybe I should try talking to a linguistic expert—"

"Leia," I interrupted, by now growing lightheaded, "*just guess what I am*!"

"A penguin!"

Will this never end?

"An adoring crowd praising the awesomeness of Luna, Puppy Detective?" Creeper guessed.

He knew me too well, for I was, indeed, dramatizing a very popular event—little Luna kid fans, gathering in reverence to lavish cheers and admiring squeals on Luna, Puppy Detective.

"Correct," I announced, dropping back to all four paws. The room around me was spinning. I suddenly stumbled sideways (lots of "s" words!), my vision still blurry. "Creeper," I mumbled groggily, "I think I…spun…"

Trailing off, I started to drop onto my chin, but ended up flying backward as a stream of vomit flooded from my lips, coating the tile and a bit of my Snuggy Rug with a fresh layer of pungent puke (disgusting but nevertheless impressive "p" words!).

Creeper jumped back, alarmed. Wagging her tail some more, Leia put on her Thinking Face, as if she couldn't quite figure out why I had thrown up. By the way, Leia's Thinking Face is an expression where she scrunches up one eye, coils her mouth into one corner of her face, and tilts her head to the side. Usually when she does this, one of her ears flops over. It's sort of a goofy twist on the traditional Puppy Sad Face, only it's not a Sad Face, it's a Thinking Face.

"Mother!" Creeper gasped. Quickly correcting himself and blushing (if that's possible for a gray kitten), he amended, "I mean, *Luna*! Are you okay?"

Oh, I just love it when he calls me "Mother"!

Whenever Creeper accidentally addresses me as if I were his biological parent, it reminds me of my two dog sons, who were at an animal shelter with me when they—along with Leia—were born. A different family, however, adopted my husband and two sons, leaving me to solve mysteries all by myself with nobody but Leia as an assistant (until, of course, Creeper came along). Apparently, my husband's family had predicted Leia's chipper but clueless turnout, so they selected my two sons for their household instead.

Shaking my head, I swallowed hard, trying to get the yucky taste out of my mouth. *Ew, I hate throwing up! It's horrible for my image!*

"I'm fine," I managed weakly.

"Whoa, Mommy. You look like Emily right before she eats her oatmeal, only her oatmeal's in a bowl, and yours isn't," Leia piped up quite unhelpfully, wiping her Thinking Face away and thumping her tail. Then she grinned hopefully. "Can I eat your oatmeal, Mommy?"

I glowered at the pile of upchuck in front of me. "Go ahead, Leia. But be forewarned—it *isn't* oatmeal."

Leia put on her Thinking Face again, then carelessly leaned in and began to lap up the apparently appetizing ("a" words!) barf before her.

Hey, this way I won't get in trouble for puking, at least.

My hopes were dashed, however, when Mrs. Hickman entered the living room at that moment, carrying a clean pillowcase for one of the pillows on the downstairs sofa. She dropped the pillowcase upon beholding the scene before her, mouth open and clearly shocked.

Creeper took advantage of the situation, racing forward and grabbing one corner of the pillowcase.

He shook the fabric back and forth, enjoying the feel of the cotton sliding across his teeth.

Still standing with her eyes nearly bugged out of her head, Mrs. Hickman's glance briefly flicked to Creeper. Obviously, she wasn't sure whether to spank Creeper or me first. But by the look on her face, I could tell she knew I was the one who had tossed my lunch. It's *always* me, unfortunately.

"Bad!" Mrs. Hickman managed at last. "Luna, I told you not to eat too fast! And Creeper, you drop my clean pillowcase before I swat you!" Obediently, Creeper let the corner of the fabric go, though I silently predicted a rewashing of the pillowcase in the time that followed.

Creeper's submissive behavior didn't seem to appease Mrs. Hickman. She stomped her foot. "Ugh! Now I have to clean all this up! You know what? Outside! All of you!"

And thus began—though I didn't know it at the time—the Mystery of No-Slack Jack.

CHAPTER TWO (II, *Dos*)

I Nearly Slice and Dice Pip/Dognapped!

Outside is no fun. Not when it's early morning and the sun has barely crept over the mountains, anyway. Sunning myself isn't nearly as enjoyable as it is later in the day.

Deciding I might as well take advantage of this opportunity, however, I trotted over to the patch of grass in the center of our yard, where I promptly *relieved myself* and went to relax in the shade of the porch. I'm funny that way—when the sun isn't available, I take the cool shade.

Immediately, Leia began plodding about, chasing dragonflies, butterflies, bumblebees, and flies all across the small yard, her silky ears flapping out behind her like a victory banner, her chub jiggling all the way. As she ran, she sang for the whole neighborhood:

"First a game of Canine Checkers;
That was fun!
That was fun!
Then a bit of Butterfly-Catchers;
On the run!
On the run!"

Leia thinks she's a real song whiz, but I personally prefer Pawthoven. At any rate, she isn't a good singer, even by the most lax standards in the world.

Then, at that moment, I was distracted from Leia's screechy song by a purring above me. "*Luuuuuuuuuuuna.*"

I grimaced, squinting to look up at Pip the Siamese cat, who had positioned herself conveniently just out of my reach on top of the block fence. "Scram, Pip," I commanded sharply. I really wasn't in the mood for cats at that moment.

Pip grinned. "Make me, *Luna.*"

I blinked, seriously shocked ("s" words!). Had Pip just challenged my queenly reign over my house—scratch that—*this whole neighborhood* without reason or authority? *Ooh, she's asking for it!*

I squared my queenly shoulders and flashed my glistening yellow teeth (which are also quite queenly—"q" words!). "Care to repeat that, you sniveling, stuck-up little furball?"

Widening her eyes, Pip stretched her front legs, trying to appear seriously offended. "Why, *Luna,* what an *insult* you have just *hurled* ruthlessly at me! Aren't we *friends?*"

"No," I said shortly.

"Scat, you lowdown, good-for-nothing, double-crossing, troublemaking *loser,*" Creeper snarled, leaping to his feet. His eyes narrowed as they zeroed in on Pip.

"Wha…? *Creeper*! To think you are capable of such *language*!" gasped Pip.

"That's not the only thing I'm capable of. I seem to recall an incident a couple of weeks ago when you went flying off the fence, screaming like a kitten," Creeper jeered. He was, of course, referring to the occasion in *Luna: Puppy Detective #1: Catnapped!,* my first mystery, when he leapt up and scared Pip from her precarious perch (you guessed it—"p" words!) atop the fence. After that, many Pip scares had taken place, to my amusement and to Pip's annoyance (but I don't care what Pip thinks).

Pip's lip curled, yet I did see her inch back just a bit, wary of future attacks on Creeper's part. "Oh, well, before I go, *Luna,* I want to give you a little *present.*"

"I don't want any presents from you, street garbage."

"Speaking of garbage…" Pip leaned down deliberately, retching so long and so loud that at first I didn't get what she was doing. Then it hit me.

Literally.

A big, fat, fuzzy, goopy *hairball* dropped through the air, straight onto—*NO!*—my queenly forehead!

"EEEEEEEEEK!" I squealed, running around in circles. "Egh! Cat germs! Get it off! Get it *off*!"

"Oh, cool. A ball," cried Leia, temporarily halting her butterfly chasing to marvel at the scene before her. "Can we play toss, Mommy?"

"I will tear the whiskers out of your face!" Creeper threatened, soaring through the air and landing on the fence. Pip leapt to the side, wobbling a bit but managing to keep her balance. She hissed, and her claws popped out of her paws.

Creeper dove for Pip, and the chase was on. She raced along the fence line, turned a corner, and scurried down the other fence toward the gate leading out of my yard. After shaking the hairball off my head, I ran along the fence to keep up with her. That meant, of course, my eyes were focused upward, on the crooked crook of a cat. That also meant, unfortunately, my eyes *weren't* focused *forward*, and therefore *not* on the horribly hard wood-and-metal gate…

BANG!

"OOF!"

I slumped down onto the rocks, my head spinning. I felt about ready to upchuck for the second time that day. *For goodness' sake, who put that gate there? Egh!*

"Creeper, the gate!" I managed weakly as Pip flung herself into the rocks in the front yard, racing away toward the driveway.

In a single movement, Creeper landed on the gate, used his claws to unlatch it, and leapt off, causing the gate to swing open. *Well, he could've done that a bit sooner. But no matter.*

I sprang to my paws and skittered out of the backyard in the direction of the driveway. Behind me, I heard Leia exclaim, "Mommy, where are you going?" I ignored her. I had more important things to do than explain the important things I had to do to Leia, who most likely wouldn't understand the importance of the important things I had to do, so logically, talking to Leia wasn't very high on my list of important things to do.

Slicing and dicing Pip, however, ranked pretty high on that list, and I was in the process of executing said slicing and dicing. I dashed forward, my queenly ears flowing behind me in the wind, as my paws touched down on the driveway. By this time, Creeper was some ways ahead of me, and Pip had scrambled up onto the Hickman car, jumped into the street, and then scurried across to the opposite sidewalk.

Creeper paused when he reached the road, breathing hard. Screeching to a stop beside him,

I stared at the gloomy street. "Cross?" I asked, inquiring if Creeper was up to the challenge or not.

Creeper nodded. "I'm game if you are."

I crouched down low, looking both ways. "I'm game." Springing into the air, I scrambled across the asphalt, my breath quickening in panic. From puppyhood, I had been taught two things: One, Jesus is Lord, and He loves little Shih Tzu sleuths like me. Two, *avoid roads at all costs.* A rampaging vehicle killed my husband's father. I didn't want to be next.

Ooh, suspense is building. Does Luna get smushed like yesterday's bubble gum or does she not? Will the world-famous Shih Tzu detective live to do her world-famous Shih Tzu detecting another day?

Well, you probably already guessed the answer—Luna, Puppy Detective, survived! Okay, I'll give you a second to breathe sighs of relief, applaud, and plan future parties to celebrate this news.

One.

Okay, now that that's over with, back to the story.

My pawnails collided with the pavement of the sidewalk on the other side of the street at the exact moment Creeper's did, and also at the exact moment

Pip screeched and darted along the sidewalk toward who-knows-where.

"After that kitty-kitty!" I shouted, rocketing madly for the irritating cat with Creeper right on my queenly paws.

"*Na-na-na-na-na-na,*" sang Pip tauntingly, zooming around a corner. Creeper and I followed, our eyes narrowed in determination.

"Coward!" I returned somewhat lamely, because I had started to huff and puff.

NO, little Luna kid fans, I am *NOT* fat. I'm not even *slightly* overweight. It's just that I don't place much value on physical exercise. Generally, my everyday life doesn't involve running up and down sidewalks like a street dog being chased by the dog-catcher.

We shot like fluffy bullets around several more corners, keeping Pip in sight. She held a considerable lead, but Creeper, streaking forward like a Greyhound, almost caught her tail. Despite all my queenly efforts, I was now eating Creeper's dust as he zipped ahead, bent on de-nosing Pip.

"Get her, Creeper! Get her!" I yapped, and then, for some odd reason, Creeper suddenly screeched to a halt—which meant I slammed quite forcefully into his rear end. *Oh, my nose! My queenly nose! This is even worse for my reputation!* "What?" I managed, shaking my head. Creeper had, as I previously mentioned, stopped dead in his tracks. He appeared to be gazing up at a big, hulking, pit bull-sized…pit bull. *Oh, joy.* Pip, having also abruptly reduced her speed, skidded to the side, scaled a nearby house's roof, and was gone.

Curling his lip, the silver pit bull stared down at us, the white patch on his belly looking more like an endless vacuum about ready to swallow one queenly Shih Tzu in particular. Behind him stood two Miniature Bull Terriers, who were also pit bulls, as "pit bull" refers to a number of breeds (the silver one was an American Staffordshire Terrier). One of the Mini Bull Terriers was white, and the other one was white and brown. My attention, however, moved from them to their silver leader when the American Staffordshire Terrier barked, "What are you doing down here?"

I don't like the looks of these guys. They have "street dog" written all over them, with fifty-five million exclamation marks at the end. What to do…what to do…

"What a nice day," I commented shakily—er, *stupendously*—as I squared my shoulders. I needed to look tough to show these boneheaded bozos ("b" words!) that they couldn't cross Luna, Puppy Detective, and get away with it.

"Grr," Creeper added, and he meant it. He popped out his claws and swiped the air in front of his face as a warning.

"A couple of troublemakers, eh?" piped up the white-and-brown Mini Bull Terrier.

"Can we get 'em, Jake? Can we? Oh can we, *please*?" drooled the white Mini Bull Terrier.

"First, a question." The American Staffordshire Terrier leaned down so his nose almost touched mine. "What're you runts doing around here?"

I immediately said the first thing that came to my mind. "Painting."

The pit bull's blue eyes squinted. "*Painting*?" he echoed blankly.

"Yes, that's right," I affirmed, standing up straighter and puffing out my chest. "We're painting. See, this neighborhood, if you ask me, is a bit of a fixer-upper, hardly worthy of housing an amazing Shih Tzu sleuth such as myself. Therefore, I decided to come down here and do some...painting. Yeah, I was thinking some mango for those trellises over there, a sort of peach for the main structures, with some violet for the trim?" *Hmm. Not a bad idea. I'll have to talk to the Hickmans about having my house redone. Wait! They can't understand me. Ah, well. Maybe I could just write them a note. Wait! No opposable thumbs. This just isn't my day, is it?*

The pit bull curled his lip, staring down at me with his glassy eyes. "Can we get 'em *now,* Jake?" drawled the white Mini Bull Terrier. "They answered the question."

The pit bull was just turning his head to respond when suddenly my queenly ears detected the roaring of an engine behind me. Before I had a chance to turn around, the brown-and-white Mini Bull Terrier shrieked, "Beat it!"

"Move, move, move!" snarled the head pit bull as the threesome whirled and rocketed away on paws like lightning.

Huh. That's weird.

"Yeah!" I shouted, completely forgetting about the noise behind me.

"Um, Luna?" Creeper quavered.

"You better run away!" I continued, showing my teeth to the air where the three pit bull losers had just been. "Nobody can withstand the shock of the presence of Luna, Puppy Detective, for very long!"

"LUNA?"

I huffed, turning to my adoptive kitten son. "What is it? I'm on a roll here."

Creeper started to speak, but then I turned and looked over my shoulder. There was a large black-and-white truck that had parked on the sidewalk not far from us. I wondered what it was doing there. Maybe the occupants of it were there to observe my awesome painting skills. *Well, that's okay. I can paint their van for them too—perhaps a nice purple color. But the very first thing to go would be the huge ANIMAL CONTROL stamped across the side. Wait…!*

I turned and bolted as a dogcatcher stepped out of the van's side door, Creeper right behind me. Just then, however, we slammed into something.

I stumbled backward, then lifted my eyes quickly and gasped out, "Leia?"

"Hi, Mommy!" chirped my chubby sidekick (she's my side*kick* because I kick her in the side when she does something wrong). "Sorry it took so long. You guys run fast. I couldn't catch up, and—"

A pair of rough hands thrust themselves downward and wrapped around my queenly waist. "No, no, no, no, no!" I wailed as I was pulled, kicking and screaming, into the air.

Creeper's fur puffed out and he hissed, arching his back. (Normally I hate it when cats arch their backs, but on Creeper, it's kind of cute.)

"Help!" I cried.

Leia put on her Thinking Face. "Is someone in danger?"

Snarling, Creeper flung himself for the dog-catcher, but tucking me under one arm, the man reached out and caught the scruff of Creeper's neck.

"Leia!" Creeper shrieked.

"Do something!" I added, twisting frantically.

Leia immediately plopped onto her behind and started to sing, "*Doing something...is a whole lot better than doing nothing...*"

At that moment, the dogcatcher turned and headed for his van, still in possession of Creeper and me! Cheerfully, Leia followed, asking innocently, "Where are we going?"

"Leia! *Get us down*!" I implored my obviously clueless daughter.

"Who's Down? Where can I find him to get him for you?" Leia asked, stopping as the dogcatcher stopped and thumping her tail.

He opened the back of the van and flung Creeper and me inside. Milliseconds later, Leia was beside us, belting out musical verses at the top of her lungs.

Then the back doors of the van slammed shut.

CHAPTER THREE (III, *Tres*)

The Sierra Sunrise Animal Care Center

The back of the truck was dark, and there was a chain-link barrier separating us from the bozo in the front seat. *Ugh! Caught by the pound! Why didn't Creeper warn me?*

"*Goin' for a road trip, on the road. Goin' for a road trip, pack a load. Goin' on a road trip, just for fun. Goin' on a road trip, done and done,*" Leia sang, her chubby front paws clunking on the surface of the floor to the so-called "rhythm" of her ridiculous tune.

At that moment, I heard a low growling just to my right. I froze. "Creeps, was that you?"

"Nope," Creeper whispered.

I scrunched up my nose. "Then who…*was* it?"

"Who goes there?" snarled a deep, gruff voice from the same direction the growl had come from.

My back legs started trembling—er, *tightening with bravery*—as I gulped—er, *growled dominantly*—and turned to face the voice. Gathering my wits and straightening heroically, I squeaked—er, *stated regally*—"I am…" Then I paused, realizing my voice was too high-pitched—er, *highly dignified for whomever I was addressing to comprehend.* Puffing out my chest, I bravely restarted, this time in a much more reasonable tone. "I am Luna, Puppy Detective, Empress of Svalbard, Queen of Hickmandom, Ruler of Sierra Vista, and Monarch of the World. To whom am I speaking?"

"Name's Buster," the speaker—who I assumed was a dog—replied from the darkness. His voice was laced with a heavy tough-dog accent, so that when he said "Buster," it sounded like "Busta." "I'm a Tibetan Mastiff. The name's Buster, as I said, and if ya take one more step, I'm gonna bust ya, Miss Lola, Puggy Incentive."

"I'm *Luna, Puppy Detective,*" I corrected importantly. Honestly! If he was going to question my fighting skills, he should at least question *my* fighting skills, not some *Lola, Puggy Incentive's*!

"Hi," Leia chirped, suddenly interested in the conversation quickly unfolding. "I'm Leia! I think

Buster is a nice name. I like Tibetan Mastiffies, too! They're *big*! Bigger than big ol' hambuggers!"

"Leia, it is pronounced *hamburgers,* and Tibetan Mastiffs are *NOT* cute," I told my daughter seriously. "Especially not *this* one. He sounds like a street dog to me."

"Yes, and I look ten times worse," Buster promised from the darkness. "And I could make *you* look ten times worse than how *I* look ten times worse, so stay away."

"Yes, sir," Creeper said instantly, saluting.

"What?" I demanded. "Creeper, this bonehead is questioning my queenly rule over him! If I command him to grovel at my paws and kiss my queenly toes, who is he to refuse?" I pivoted, staring into the blackness. "Now, bonehead, grovel at my paws and kiss my queenly toes!"

"Uh…no."

"You're right. You're unworthy," I informed him plainly. Well, at least he had a half-decent head on his shoulders. Even in the dim light, he could recognize a worthy queen when he saw one.

"And I'm Mocha," added another, more feminine voice from behind me. I whirled, my heart beginning to pound louder and faster. "I'm part

Border collie and part pit bull. And this is my Beagle friend, Benson."

Processing this, I immediately deduced that we were in the presence of several canines. The real question, however, was much more serious: Were they friend or foe?

"Is that a cat?" yapped the Beagle, Benson.

"Cat?" Creeper looked over his shoulder, as if wondering if a feline had snuck up behind him. Then he looked back at the space where he judged Benson to be. "Well, *technically*, I'm a cat. But *metaphorically*, no, I'm not." Creeper bent down in a play bow. He gave off a series of short, excited yips.

"Creeper, this is hardly the time for puppy play," I reprimanded him.

"I agree," concurred Mocha solemnly. I heard her sink onto the floor of the truck and heave an ominous sigh. "To think about where we're headed just gives me the chills."

A stone dropped to the bottom of my stomach (though I don't specifically remember devouring any rocks as of recent). "The pound?" I asked fearfully—er, *firmly and professionally*.

"Not quite," Buster jumped in. Leia, Creeper, and I turned to face the patch of darkness where he was. "We're headed to the Sierra Sunrise Animal Care Center. It's no-kill, but it's also bad news for all of us. We have to sit in cages all day, and we only get certain amounts of food."

Leia started shaking. "But I'm just a little Boo-Boo! Boo-Boos need to eat!" Leia's habit of calling herself a "Boo-Boo" is a bit annoying, but I've learned to ignore it. Besides, I had better things to focus on.

"Yeah," Buster continued, as if trying to purposefully spook us. "They close you in a small room, only letting you out to take you for a five-minute stroll. Then they give you a tiny dish filled with kibble, and when you're finished, they give you a...*bath.*"

Buster let his last word drag out, and silence fell over the whole van. *Bath! Baths are the worst thing since shock collars! And even worse—they were invented before shock collars! What is this world coming to?*

I didn't want to go to this Sierra Sunrise place, not at all! I wanted to go home to my Snuggy Rug, flop down, suck my dewclaw, and take a nap! Naps are much better than baths! I didn't want to go, I didn't want to go, I didn't want to go...!

"They'll never take me alive," I declared through my teeth.

"*They will never take me alive,*" Leia sang, spinning in a gleeful circle, completely oblivious as to the gravity of our present predicament ("p" words!). "*I do not take anyone's bribe. They will never take me alive*!" I huffed as Leia giggled. Apparently, there was no conviction behind her words of resolve.

"And it's even worse since the ghost has been showing up," Benson piped up at that moment.

I wheeled around. "*Ghost?*"

Immediately, Benson opened his mouth to explain, but just then, the van stopped, and the dog-catcher hopped out, flinging the back doors of the van open. I narrowed my eyes.

"Stay away from me, you poor excuse for a dog-napper!" I snarled at the man as he reached in and seized Benson's waist.

"Rrr," Benson growled, but the man paid him no mind, tucking him under one arm and reaching for me.

Oh, no you don't!

I slid out of the way, near the corner where Buster lurked. Buster, showing me his large, rather sharp teeth, snapped his jaws just inches from my tail. *Gulp. That was a little too close for comfort.*

If it came down to being stuck with Buster or the dogcatcher, I would probably choose the dogcatcher. That way, at least I would stay alive. Still, if I could somehow get past the dogcatcher…

I scrambled forward, trying to jump out of the truck to the side, but the dogcatcher hooked a leash over my head just before I did, so I ended up on the pavement, as planned, but still the dogcatcher's victim, as *not* planned.

A few moments later, I heard Creeper hiss, then yowl, then let out a loud caterwaul: "*YI! HISS! YIP-YIP-YIP HISS!*"

But alas, even the fierceness of Creeper's cat yammering didn't disturb the dopey dogcatcher ("d" words!). "Come on, kitty," he muttered, snagging the scruff of Creeper's neck and managing to get another leash on my kitten son.

I rose up on my hind legs, batting the man's pants in protest. "You put my son down!" I snarled. "I will slice you and dice you and ice you and anything-else-that-ends-with-'ice' you!"

The dogcatcher apparently wasn't scared of being sliced, diced, iced, and anything else that ends with "iced," because he ignored me. Shocking, right? Let me just say that again—*he ignored me*! Me, Luna,

Puppy Detective, queen of the entire earth and—I hasten to add—of *him*! And HE IGNORED ME! One more time, just so all you little Luna kid fans can process what I'm saying—*HE IGNORED ME!*

Ugh! What an insult!

"There's only one way to get out of this," Benson announced as the dogcatcher got Leia on a leash, then slammed the van doors shut, apparently deciding that three canines and a struggling cat were quite enough. Mocha and Buster, left inside the van for the dogcatcher's second trip, began yapping and scratching on the walls.

"What's that?" I asked, desperately trying to cling to the asphalt of the parking lot I found myself on. But, as I'm sure you know, little Luna kid fans, claws and asphalt don't really like each other, so I ended up sliding backward, my queenly nose stuck in the air defiantly. Nobody, not even Emily, could walk *me* successfully, and I wasn't about to let myself be walked into an *animal shelter*, of all places!

Behind me, I knew there was a large building. I could smell several dogs and cats that had recently taken the same route I was being forced to take.

"Dazzle him with your cuteness so he'll adopt you on the spot and spare you the horrors of the cage,"

Benson explained. He leaned in and began caressing the dogcatcher's cheek with his rough tongue. "Ah, you're a good little human. Aren't I so cute?"

"I'm not going to lower myself to sucking up to this peabrained pooch-snatcher," I informed Benson seriously, gritting my teeth. "Besides, I already *have* an owner, and this dogcatcher's not even worthy to hold my leash, let alone 'adopt' me, so why would I bother?"

"Peacocks."

I squinted, losing precious friction as my muscles relaxed and I slid a few feet closer to the building. Leia had been the one to speak. She was trotting obediently beside the dogcatcher, but she turned to look back at me with an adoring expression. "What?" I asked.

"Peacocks. You said they were called peagrains. But I said peacocks, which is what they are. Or peahens, which are the females," Leia explained, somewhat thoughtfully.

"First of all, it's pea*brains,* Leia, and second of all, we have to get out of here before we're taken into the place of no return!" I exploded at my daughter. "So do you care to *help*?"

"Oh, what a good little dogcatchie you are," crooned Benson, imitating human baby talk and still licking the dogcatcher's cheek.

"Ew!" exclaimed the dogcatcher, trying to nudge Benson away with his shoulder. "Stop it, you gross dog!"

"Ugh! I can't believe he didn't fall for that," Benson grumbled, settling back away from the man's face and pouting.

"Must be a cat person," Creeper theorized in a very professor-like way, holding up one paw importantly.

"Pee on his shoe!" Leia recommended, bouncing with each chipper step. "Humans *love* that!"

Benson looked down questioningly at my daughter. Leia had just suggested the act of urinating on the dogcatcher's shoe, which obviously wasn't an option for Benson, who sat tucked underneath the dogcatcher's arm and well out of the way of the human's boot.

Kicking and screaming, I glanced over my shoulder at that instant, realizing the dogcatcher was heading for the side door of the shelter. He opened it with a bit of difficulty and then hauled all four of us inside. Curious, I paused in my struggles to glance around me. We appeared to be in a hallway lined with cages, most of which were filled with dogs and cats.

One, an albino Doberman pinscher (which means he was all white with pink eyes), licked his lips as we passed by. My paws were still planted firmly on the smooth concrete flooring, but they didn't seem to be helping me halt much.

Huffing and puffing from the effort of trying to control Leia, Creeper, Benson, and me all at the same time, the dogcatcher finally stopped, straining as he opened one cage with a spotted Dalmatian already in it. Nudging Leia and me with his foot, the dogcatcher yanked the leashes free, but just as I was whirling to de-nose the dognapping doofus, he slammed the cage door shut and locked it tight.

"Why, I oughta…" grumbled Creeper angrily. He hissed, lifting his paw to scratch the man's leg.

"Ow!" yelped the man quite girlishly. "Stinking cat!"

"Must be a hamster person," Benson mused as the man grabbed Creeper by the scruff of his neck, hoisting him up into the air.

"Grr!" I snarled, flinging myself at the bars of the cage. "Get your hands off my cat! Rrr, woof, woof!"

I began yapping at the top of my lungs, hopping up and down with each dignified bark.

In case you little Luna kid fans don't know, my beautiful bark ("b" words!) is a precious and much-exercised gift from God, who designed me with such a roaring voice of regal authority that not even the toughest dognapping dope can withstand the sheer pressure of its awesomeness. Leia will tell you that my bark resembles a squeaking field mouse with a tummy ache, but that's just Leia's way of saying it's the best bark she's ever heard. No, really!

Now, prepare yourselves, because this next detail is a *really* big shock.

THE BOZO IGNORED ME AGAIN!

I narrowed my eyes as the dogcatcher stomped away, Creeper and Benson in his custody, out of my sight. I yapped some more. I spun in a frustrated circle. I pounded on the chain-link door. I snarled my threats. I bared my teeth. I slammed my paws repeatedly on the newspapers covering the floor of the cage. I screamed. I kicked. I hit whatever was within reach. I chased my tail. I caught it and shook it back and forth. I fake fainted.

But nothing helped, and soon the dogcatcher had caged Creeper and Benson, then headed back outside for Mocha and Buster.

"Wow, you're nuts," commented the white-and-black Dalmatian standing at the far corner of the spacious area.

Breathing hard from my outburst, I turned, my teeth still showing, as I glared at the dog and Leia. "Don't talk to me right now," I snapped. "In fact, don't talk to me *ever*. I'm Queen Luna. Talk to me, and you may very well be punished by vanishing into thin air—*poof*! Or I might turn you into a frog."

"Ooh, ooh, ooh! Can you turn me into a penguin?" Leia asked excitedly, jumping up and down. Her chubby ears flopped back and forth, and her tail wagged ecstatically. "I want to be a penguin! Penguin! Penguin! Penguin!"

"No, Leia, no penguin."

Leia stopped jumping. "No...penguin?" Eyes wide, she evidently couldn't believe what she was hearing.

"That's right, Leia. No penguin."

Leia burst into tears. "But, Mommy! The cute little cuddly penguin—"

"We can talk about cute little cuddly penguins when we're out of here, Leia," I interrupted, turning to face the cage door.

"Who are you?" asked the Dalmatian, her tail wagging slightly.

"Shh," I shushed the spotted canine. "I'm not here to talk to you. In fact, I'm not supposed to be *here* at all. I'm owned. I have a home. *I'm not a stray.*"

The Dalmatian grinned in that goofy way that Dalmatians grin. "Cool. I'm owned, too. My name is Darling. I belong to the Jensons."

"That's fantastic, but *I don't care,*" I spat disgustedly. "I do not associate with lowly Dalmatians."

Darling glanced at me, then glanced at her long legs, as if wondering how I could call her "lowly." I snorted. Apparently this dog didn't understand the concept of metaphors.

"Luna!" I suddenly heard Creeper caterwaul from nearby. I couldn't see him, but I shoved my ear up against the side of the cage in the general direction of where his voice had come from.

"Creeps! You okay?"

"Yeah, yeah! I'm fine. How's Leia?"

I glanced over my shoulder at my chubby daughter, who was humming and spinning carelessly in little ballerina circles around the cage with her plump paws flailing.

"She's okay, too, I guess. A little *too* okay," I muttered, huffing as I plopped onto my royal rear ("r" words!).

Bobbing her head up and down to Leia's ridiculous tune, Darling began lifting her front paws and drumming on the floor of the cage to give Leia more of a beat. "Listen up, you two," I snarled, spinning to face Darling and Leia, "we are in a dire situation. I don't know if you know this, *Darling*, but I am a very important, world-famous Shih Tzu sleuth, and I need to get back to my home!"

"Good luck with that," mumbled Darling, still drumming.

Poor dog. She doesn't realize there's no such thing as luck.

Darling continued, "Hardly anyone who ever walks in here is an owner looking for a dog. Consider this a fresh start."

My eyes widened. "'A fresh start'?! No, no, no, I'm going back to Emily, and no one can stop me! I am Luna, Puppy Detective, and I would walk across forests, swim through rivers, fight venomous snakes, and tightrope over boiling lava to get back to my family!"

"Yeah!" Leia agreed, dropping onto her large behind and beginning to scratch one of her ears. Then she scrunched up her nose, staring at me blankly. "Wait, did you just say *lava*?"

A hiss of irritated air escaped through my teeth. *Ugh, doesn't anyone care about getting out of here?*

Darling shrugged. "Well, maybe you can get out tonight. Sometimes the security dogs come and let us out of the cages. Then, while nobody's looking, you can slip away, back to your family. I'll create a distraction." Glumly, Darling suddenly cast her eyes to the floor. "If the *ghost* isn't distraction enough, that is."

CHAPTER FOUR (IV, *Cuatro*)

The Ghost of No-Slack Jack

"Ghost?" I asked inquisitively, my queenly ears immediately going on the alert. "What ghost?"

Sighing, Darling plopped down onto her spotted behind and explained, "Well, see, there used to be this dog in the shelter. He was an old street fighter known only as No-Slack Jack. He was rumored to have escaped the shelter, but died soon afterward. Now his ghost haunts this place at night."

My eyes widened with interest. Leia crouched down on the ground, quivering. "A g-ghost?" she stammered. A wet puddle formed on the newspaper beneath her. I rolled my eyes.

"Leia, ghosts aren't real," I told her seriously.

"Oh, the ghost is real, all right."

I jerked my head toward the new voice. Directly opposite my cage, a Maine Coon (which is a type of cat—*egh*!) stared out at me from behind a chain-link door, her gaze intense. The cat's coat was a brownish-orange color with black stripes, and her eyes were a glowing green except for small black slits that ran down the center.

Shaking off my surprise at hearing the cat speak, I puffed out my chest and demanded, "Oh, and how would *you* know if the ghost is real or not? Until Luna, Puppy Detective, has dubbed something dangerous or harmless, it is not to be considered either."

The cat turned in a circle, picking up her right paw and stroking it lovingly with her rough pink tongue. "The ghost is restless," seethed the feline, twitching her tail. Above me, I heard Creeper shifting his weight.

Hmm. He must be listening, too.

"Why, just the other night, he kept us up with his howling. He's death itself. Haven't you ever *heard* of the legend of No-Slack Jack?" The cat licked her lips, staring at me hard.

I huffed indignantly. "Only *death* is death itself, you misinformed mischief-maker!" Suddenly, I grinned. "Although even *you* must be able to recognize great alliteration when you hear it. Please, hold your applause. No, no, really, that's okay. I've already heard how awesome I am from about twenty billion little Luna kid fans. You can just stand in awed silence. That's fine."

The cat tilted her head. "Who did you say you were?"

"Luna, Puppy Detective."

The cat blinked. "I've never heard of you."

I huffed again. "Well, then you're not a very informed cat, are you? Except on the matters of make-believe ghosts, that is."

Annoyed, the Maine Coon narrowed her eyes. "I just told you the ghost is real."

I turned my nose up at her snootily. "Well, *I* just told *you* the ghost *isn't* real, and since I am Luna, Puppy Detective, and I'm famous and all that, I am therefore considered more trustworthy in a court of law."

"This isn't a court of law."

"Of course it isn't. Who said it was?"

"You did."

"Ha! I did not! Just one more reason to consider you a lying lowlife," I announced triumphantly, grinning from ear to ear.

Suddenly, a loud *gong-gong-gong-gong*ing sounded, and Darling's ears pricked. "It's four o'clock P.M., Mountain Standard Time," the Dalmatian whispered.

"Closing time," another animal added from a cage out of my range of vision.

"Ghost time," the Maine Coon snarled eerily.

"Suppertime?" Leia suggested hopefully, thumping her tail.

I whirled on Darling and Leia, proclaiming grandly, "*Escape* time!"

A full half hour passed by before the three security dogs—Spot, Spike, and Specks—came into view. All three were Labradors, tall and muscular, wearing navy blue vests with SIERRA SUNRISE SECURITY stitched onto the sides, along with the logo of a sun rising over a pink cat and a purple dog. ("Sierra Sunrise Security" is horrible alliteration, by the way. *HORRIBLE!*)

"Hey, Spot!" called the Maine Coon. "Hey, be a sport and let me out, will ya?"

"No way, Cat-Eyes," growled the black Lab called Spot.

"*Creep*-Eyes is more like it," put in Spike, the yellow Lab.

The chocolate Lab, Specks, didn't say anything as the threesome approached my cage. I waved my paws to get the attention of the bozos. "Hey, hey! I am Luna, Puppy Detective, and I demand an immediate release from this unthinkably unreasonable enclosure!"

"What's an *exposure*?" asked Leia.

"*Enclosure*," I spat.

"*Impose your*? That's an incomplete thought, Mommy. That doesn't make any sense," Leia pointed out, grinning from ear to chubby ear.

Ugh. Leia will never learn.

"Hey, look. It's a new dog," exclaimed Spot. He lifted his jet-black paw and flipped the latch on our cage.

Shoving the door open, I skittered out onto the concrete flooring of the aisle, shaking off. *Ah, it's good to be free.*

Leia plodded out of the cage right behind me, still grinning. "Now that we're out, Mommy, can we play Hide-and-Seek?"

"No."

"I Spy?"

"No."

"Duck-Duck-Goose?"

"No."

"Leapdog?"

"*NO.*"

Leia put on her Thinking Face. Then she thumped her tail. "Okay, Mommy."

I glanced back at Darling, who had bounded out right behind me. She winked as the Labradors moved on to let a few other animals out of their cages.

When they got to Creeper's, I looked up and saw Creeper whine like a dog, then yip. Chuckling, Specks flipped the latch, and Creeper dropped down beside me.

"What's the plan?" he whispered.

"We're ditching this dump when Darling creates a diversion," I whispered back.

"Look! A squeaky ball!" cried Darling suddenly, whirling and dashing for the opposite end of the hall.

"A squeaky ball?" exclaimed all the cats and dogs present, even the security bozos.

I grinned, then whirled and sprinted for the side door exit. "Creeper, get up on the knob," I commanded, screeching to a halt just inches in front of the door. Leia waddled up behind me, singing softly under her breath about escapes, grapes, and movie tapes. I guess she didn't realize how serious the situation had become.

But before Creeper could make a move, a ghostly white figure stepped into our path.

CHAPTER FIVE (V, *Cinco*)

Ghost Attack

"AAAAAAAAH!" Leia shrieked, ducking down and covering her head with her plump paws ("p" words!).

As for me, I had frozen dead still, my eyes as big as bowling balls, staring at the marvel before me. I don't believe in ghosts. I never have. Ghosts are the stuff of creepy bedtime stories, not reality. And yet, there before me, loomed a *ghost*!

The phantom was large, with four legs, a tail, and glowing white eyes. It was wrapped tightly with white cloth like a mummy, and two wings, also wrapped, extended from its eerie shoulders. Glowing mysteriously, the ghost took a step forward, opening bright red jaws and letting out a roar that came from everywhere and nowhere all at once.

Then I noticed something odd about the way the ghost moved. *It wasn't walking on the ground, but floating in midair!*

"Oh, boy," I muttered. I pivoted to run with Creeper, but realized Leia wasn't budging. "Leia!" I shouted frantically, racing over to my daughter. Creeper turned and unsheathed his claws, prepared to defend Leia and me. "It's a ghost! Run!"

"I like toast, Mommy," Leia exclaimed, perking up. She grinned and thumped her tail, scratching at a flea. "Is there toast somewhere? Is it beyond that huge, scary door? It's huge and scary, Mommy."

You've got to be kidding me. Leia doesn't even see the ghost? She's scared of the door? UGH!

"Not *toast,* Leia—*ghost!*" I repeated, slamming my shoulder into Leia's in an attempt to make her move. It didn't work.

"Boast? It's not nice to boast, Mommy, unless you're boasting in God." Leia puffed out her chest, oblivious to the danger lurking just two feet ahead of her.

"LEIA!" I finally kicked my sidekick in the side to get her attention. She sprang to her paws and, upon seeing the ghost, grinned.

"Hi, Mr. Ghost, sir. How do you do?" asked my daughter politely.

"*Run,* Leia!"

"What? Oh, okay. Guess I have to go, Mr. Ghost."

As the ghost floated forward, shrieking eerily, Creeper, Leia, and I bolted for the far end of the hall, away from our escape to the outside world. We ended up colliding with Darling. "What are you…? I thought you guys were supposed to high-tail it now," Darling muttered, whirling around to face us. Then her jaw dropped. "The ghost of No-Slack Jack!" she shouted for all the shelter to hear. "RUUUUUUUUN!"

All animals outside their enclosures scattered, and the ones left in their cages covered their eyes with their paws and retreated to the far walls. I half expected to hear Buster squeal in fright, but I didn't. In fact, I didn't see Buster anywhere. *Ah, well. Maybe he's just hiding like a cowardly coward.*

Only one dog (besides myself, of course) seemed to be brave through all of this—the albino Doberman, who lunged forward, snapping at the chain-link on the front of his cage, for the Labs had not let him out. His teeth locked on the door, and he yanked back forcefully and tore an entire section of chain-link off the front end. Then, scrambling through the hole, he dove for the ghost.

Next, something *really* weird happened.

The ghost leapt up into the air, soaring high above our heads.

"The ghost of No-Slack Jack wants revenge!" shouted a voice that sounded from all directions. I assumed it was the ghost speaking. "Now you will all pay! I will keep you trapped here forever!"

"Rex is out!" yapped a nearby Pomeranian suddenly, referring to the albino Doberman. "Hide!"

If the animals were scared of the ghost, they were terrified of Rex. "Wait a minute!" whined the ghost of No-Slack Jack as one cat started to scale a row of cages. She hopped into one and pulled the door shut as Rex's large snout appeared in front of her. "Pay attention! I'm *still* making threats!"

In fact, nobody was paying attention. Spot was racing about wildly, attempting in vain to calm everyone down. Darling was spinning in circles, chasing her tail. Rex had dissected another cage door and was shaking a squealing cat back and forth in his jaws. Leia was hopping about, singing the "Penguin Song." Creeper was clambering up cages, trying to get to the ghost's level. And, as for me…I was royally and heroically guarding the inside of my cage under the newspaper, in the off chance the ghost wanted to steal the water bowl or something.

"You all will feel my wrath!" the ghost promised. "Even the toughest of dogs here will be begging for mercy! Mark my words!"

With that, the ghost soared up, up, up, over a row of cages, and disappeared from sight.

Everyone jumped, staring after it for a moment. I wiggled out from under the newspaper and jogged to the center of the aisle, casting my eyes upward. Nothing. The ghost of No-Slack Jack was gone!

CHAPTER SIX (VI, *Seis*)

I Fidd a Buddh of Fur (I Find a Bunch of Fur)

"Luna!" Creeper called, descending rapidly through the air from the cage where he had been perched and landing neatly on his soft kitten paws. "Are you okay?"

I turned my nose up at him. "I'm Luna, Puppy Detective. Nothing can make me be *not* okay."

Leia will tell you that a puddle of yellow appeared underneath me at that moment, my back legs started trembling, and my tail tucked, but she's completely and utterly crazy, so just ignore her. Got it? Good. On with the story.

I fixed my gaze on Creeper. "Could you see much of the ghost from where you were?"

"Not more than you could see. I was trying to pounce on it, but it flew away before I could," Creeper reported, frustrated.

Suddenly, a gigantic snout thrust itself toward my back. I whirled and found myself staring into two massive pink eyes. Rex the Doberman pinscher. *I'm dead.*

"Hello. Nice day—er, *night*—eh?" I managed, wagging my tail.

"Listen, runt. I'm not one to shred a dog without reason, but you're getting on my nerves with your snooty attitude. Watch yourself," growled Rex.

I narrowed my eyes and puffed out my chest. Sure, he was a big, tough, bloodthirsty Doberman. Sure, I was a twelve-pound, snooty, lap-loving Shih Tzu. But Rex had questioned my queenly authority over him, and it was time he learned his lesson.

But he spoke before I could. "Watch yourself, runt," he repeated, "or you'll find you aren't able to watch anything anymore." With that, he turned and slunk away in that slinking way that Dobermans slink.

Gulp.

Calmly, Creeper reached over and nudged my shoulder. "Don't let him bother you, Luna. Let's check out the crime scene," my kitten son suggested.

"Rex is *sooo* nice," Leia chirped as we wheeled and hurried for the end of the hall, where the ghost had appeared near the side door. "He reminds me of that sweet Dobyman that lives in that one neighborhood Emily's always walking us in. Remember, Mommy?"

"Yes, Leia, I remember," I said through clenched teeth. You see, there's this Doberman pinscher—who isn't an albino—that Leia has a gigantic crush on for some reason. Being Leia, she finds something cute about his horrendous roar of a bark, his flashing fangs, and his gigantic paws pounding ruthlessly on the rickety old gate of his yard. Fortunately, I think he's always chained up, so he can never get out to hurt us. Still, it gives me the chills just thinking about him.

At that moment, we arrived at the spot near the side door where the ghost had appeared and chased us—"us" being Creeper and Leia, with me escorting them to safety, *not* running away.

I immediately did what all good detectives do. I put my schnauzer to the concrete and started to sniff. What did I smell? Let's see…

CONCRETE. CONCRETE. CONCRETE.

Wow, there sure is a lot of...well...concrete in this animal shelter, isn't there? I took a few steps forward, determined to smell something other than the substance making up the structure of the floor. And then I smelled it.

Well, sort of.

There was a large, smooth tuft of black fur directly in front of me, and when I sniffed...Well, you get the idea. The fur went up my nose!

Sneezing and wheezing, I managed to blow the fur out, though it was now covered in royal mucus, I'm afraid. "Oh doh," I moaned in a nasally tone quite unbecoming for a queenly dog such as myself. "Dow we cad't dmell it!" *Egh!* Every time I spoke, my N's and S's sounded like D's!

"Ooh, ooh! Are you talking penguin?" Leia asked excitedly, thumping her tail. "I can talk penguin, too! Ready? *Chirpity-chirp, chirpity-chirp-chirp-wellawee-chirp-chirpadee.*"

"Hudh up," I snapped impatiently.

"Luna, are you okay?" Creeper questioned skeptically.

I whirled on him and stomped one paw impatiently. "Do I doudd okay? That dtinking furball flew up my dose add ruided my dmelling!"

"Wait." Creeper leaned down and examined the snot-covered fuzzball. "This is a bunch of black fur. *Right here where the ghost appeared.*"

"Doh?" I demanded, sticking out my lower lip.

"So the culprit might be someone with black fur," Creeper concluded. He turned to look at Leia and me. "That's a clue as to the identity of the ghost."

I nodded in agreement. "Doh all we have to do id go dowd our checklidt of all the dogd with black fur."

Leia giggled. "You sound funny, Mommy."

"Doh I dod't," I shot back. Pivoting, I fixed my eyes on Creeper. "Doh, who all do we kdow who had black fur?"

Before Creeper could respond, Buster came bounding over, his tongue lolling lazily ("l" words!) out of his mouth. Upon seeing us, he growled, sat on his black-furred bottom, and sneered, "You puppies get away from my cage." He tapped the cage closest to the side door with a black-furred paw. "This is mine. All mine. You're not allowed to be around here." He bared his teeth and raised his black-furred hackles. "Or else I'm gonna bust ya." He swept his black-furred tail back in anticipation of what he would do to us should we choose to disobey his demands, his black-furred ears twitching.

Wait a minute. Back up. Black fur!

I snatched up the mucus-covered tuft of fur from the floor and held it up, looking from it to Buster, from it to Buster, from it to Buster, from it to Buster…

…until I finally determined that this tuft of black fur must've come from Buster. *Wow! I'm so smart.*

"Look what we foudd!" I practically shouted in the bozo's face, waving the fur tuft triumphantly. "It'd a piede of your black fur od the dcede of the crime!"

Buster scrunched up his snout. "Why are you talkin' like you don't got a nose?"

"I *do* have a dose," I yapped, by now very frustrated with the situation. I began hopping up and down to express my annoyance. "Add you have bad grammar, you peabraid!"

"Peacocks, Mommy," Leia reminded me unhelpfully.

"What are you guys talking about?" a new voice asked. It was Mocha. She strolled up, blinking at us in a friendly manner with her brown eyes. She's a Border collie/pit bull mix, if you remember, little

Luna kid fans. Mocha has the wide head shape of a pit bull but the overall coloring and fur type of a Border collie. That means she has white on her face, white paws, and a white tail tip, but long black fur on the rest of her body. Her coat is actually quite pretty.

Wait. Black fur again! Oh no! How many animals in this shelter have black fur?

I quickly thought over all the dogs I'd seen so far with black fur. First, there was Buster, obviously, then Mocha. And following her, there was Benson (though his was very short and only a patch on his back), then Darling (hers was extremely short, too), and finally, Spot the Labrador. But whom did this tuft of fur belong to?

"Creepd," I spoke at last, turning to my adoptive kitten son and making sure I was still in possession of the fur tuft. "Follow me. Let'd go back to the cage."

Creeper nodded and followed me as I slipped away, flashing a weak smile Mocha's way. She seemed like a nice dog. But I wasn't about to let myself fall into the Sweet Suspect Trap, a common maneuver used by crooked crooks. It goes like this: The criminal makes you think he/she is as harmless as a little button-nosed bunny rabbit, and then the slimy villain turns around and gets away real fast when you're not looking. Clever, yes, but not clever enough to trick Luna, Puppy Detective, that's for sure!

The instant we entered our cage, Leia plopped down and began singing, "*Penguins in the sky and air. Penguins flying everywhere. Penguins waddling on the ground. Penguins, penguins, all around*!"

I didn't bother to burst Leia's bubble by telling her that penguins were flightless birds, 'cause I had other things to do, and making Leia cease the "Penguin Song" wasn't one of them. I dropped the fur tuft on the ground in front of me, examining it closely. I didn't see anything on it that would indicate its owner, so I turned to my son.

"Okay, Creepd," I whispered, my words still marred from inhaling the black fur. Creeper nodded, leaning in so I could speak softly ("s" words!) into his ear. "I deed you to dcope thid plade out. We're going to didcover who thid fur belongd to, odde add for all."

CHAPTER SEVEN (VII, *Siete*)

My Brilliant and Heroic Plan of Action

Creeper started out of the cage first on an investigative investigation while I doused my dose (I mean, my *nose*) in water and sneezed out all of the snot clogging it up. At last, I was able to say, “Okay, Leia. Time to go help Creeps!” without it sounding like, “Okay, Leia. Time to go help Creepd!”

Leia and I jogged out into the aisle, targeting the cage nearest to the side door—Buster’s cage. We arrived just in time to hear Creeper say, “Okay, fine, fine, sure. See you.” He backed out of the cage and turned, trotting for us. “Hey, guys,” Creeper greeted.

“What’s up?” I asked, falling into step beside him.

Leia plodded along next to me, singing the “Penguin Song.” I rolled my eyes.

“Well, you know…I had to start casually,” Creeper began. I nodded. The way Creeper starts “casually” is to get down in a play bow, yip, and invite the suspect for a wrestling match. Eventually, he works some friendly conversation into it, subtly interrogating the possible criminal.

"And what did you find out?" I interjected eagerly.

"Well, Buster finally told me that he was trying to jimmy the lock on the side door when the ghost flew by," Creeper informed me, his tail wagging back and forth like that of a dog's.

I stopped. Creeper stopped. Leia kept going.

"Leia!" I hissed, and my daughter turned.

"Yes, Mommy?"

"Get back here."

"Okay, Mommy." Leia plodded goofily back to the spot where Creeper and I stood, plopping down on her bottom and thumping her tail.

Egh.

I straightened and pivoted to face Creeper, announcing proudly, "I have figured something out!" Creeper scooted closer to me in great anticipation. "Buster is *lying*!"

"Not Buster!" wailed Leia quite childishly.

I smacked a paw against my lips. "*SHHHHHH.* He could be listening," I whispered to my daughter.

Leia swept her tail across the floor and said quite loudly, "Oh, I'm sorry, Mommy!"

I rolled my eyes, then explained in a hushed voice to Creeper, "All right, the ghost appeared and flew everywhere, right? Well, where did it start?"

"By the side door," Creeper replied softly.

I nodded, smiling eagerly. What I was about to say, if you must know, little Luna kid fans, was *totally awesome.* "But who was actually at the side door, trying to jimmy the lock and escape, when that ghoulish ghoul appeared?"

Nodding in agreement with me, Creeper muttered, "*Us.*"

"So Buster couldn't have been at the door," I deduced at last, throwing one queenly paw into the air triumphantly. "Which means Buster warrants more investigation."

"Ooh! Ooh! I didn't know Buster was a warden of manipulation," Leia piped up, bouncing around in a circle. She halted suddenly and put on her Thinking Face. "What's a *warden of manipulation*?"

"Never mind, Leia."

"Buster."

I scrunched up one eye. "*What,* Leia?"

"Buster. You just said Buster was the warden of manipulation, and then you said it was Never Mind. Who is it, Mommy? Are Buster and Never Mind *both* wardens of manipulation?"

My jaw dropped. How could Leia suggest something so completely and utterly ridiculous? "Okay," I huffed, "I am striking Leia's last comment from the record for time and sanity purposes. Now, here's the plan: I will go and situate myself near the side door, which is also near Buster's cage, and watch Buster all night long. I want to see what he does."

"What if you fall asleep?" Creeper asked. "Don't you think we should do shifts instead?"

My eyelid twitched. Then I relented, "Okay, new plan. I am going to interrogate Mocha."

"Oh, Mommy!" cried Leia giddily. "Everybody knows coffee can't talk!"

I ignored her, not even bothering to put that comment on the record because I would've just removed it again. *Honestly, sometimes I worry about Leia!*

"Creeper, you stay here and watch Buster. When I return from questioning Mocha, I shall take the honorable and heroic shift of watching Buster's cage while you go talk to Rex and see what he knows—his behavior as of late is very suspicious," I finished in a very regal fashion, puffing out my chest.

Creeper raised a paw. "But Rex doesn't like cats. He doesn't really like you, either, but he might listen to you more."

I stuck my nose in Creeper's face. "You're not chicken, are you, my fine feline friend?"

Creeper went stiff. "*No.* I'm just pointing out that—"

"Blah, blah, blah," I interrupted, flapping my paws. "Get going. Buster needs watching."

Nodding obediently, Creeper slipped away, leaving me with Mrs. Short, Chubby, and Troublesome, otherwise known as Leia. Now, please note, little Luna kid fans, that I was *NOT* being cowardly in sending Creeper to go interrogate Rex. Remember, Creeper is a detective-in-training, and detectives-in-training have to see a lot of action and danger; otherwise, how will they ever learn to become an awesome sleuth like me? It was all a teaching opportunity, okay? Okay. On with the story.

"What do I do, Mommy?" Leia wanted to know, quivering as she struggled to contain her excitement.

I bopped her on the nose with my paw. "*You* get to go down to our cage and keep a close watch on the newspaper. I think someone might try to steal it."

"That's awful!" wailed Leia. "Don't worry, Mommy! I'll be the best moos-vapor guard you've ever seen!"

I huffed. "It's *newspaper*, Leia, but never mind. Just get going."

"Ooh! Ooh! Is Never Mind a moos-vapor, too? On top of being the warden of manipulation?" Leia licked her wet nose and thumped her tail.

"*Get going*," I growled.

"Sure thing, Mommy." And Leia sped away.

Turning, I pranced prissily ("p" words!) toward the cage just a few steps away, where I could hear my canine target—Mocha—snoring contentedly.

CHAPTER EIGHT (VIII, *Ocho*)

WHAT?!

When I arrived at Mocha's cage, I overheard someone saying, "Excuse me, but could you wake up, Mocha? We want to ask you a few questions about the ghost."

Instantly, I charged into the cage at top speed, my royal legs pumping and my heart pounding so hard it could've crushed nails. But then I stopped dead in my tracks.

Standing before me were the security Labradors—Spot, Spike, and Specks!

"What is going on here?" I demanded, shocked from my queenly forehead all the way down to my queenly toes.

"Whoa. Who are you?" asked Spot, turning his head to look at me.

I jumped up, slapping him across the nose and waving my front paws angrily. "I am *Luna, Puppy Detective,* if you must know, bozo, and I am working on the Case of the Ghost of No-Slack Jack, and I do not believe I authorized this interrogation!"

"Um, Luna?" Mocha asked, confused, as she got to her feet. "Why is the whole pet population of Sierra Vista suddenly crowding into my cage?"

“That’s what I’d like to know,” I returned. Then I pivoted to face the peabrained peabrains—those Labs.

“We were just in here about to talk to Mocha,” Specks explained patiently.

I jumped up, slapping him across the nose as well. I was fixing to give the brothers matching marks on each of their schnauzers.

“I *know* what you were ‘just in here about to’ do!” I stormed. Spike opened his mouth to say something, but I jumped up and slapped him across the nose, too. There. Mission accomplished. They all matched. “And I want to know *why* you were about to do it without clearance from the awesomest queenly Shih Tzu detective in the entire *WORLD*! I have paws, bucko, and I’m fixing to use them on you! Plus, I’ve got an entire army of little Luna kid fans backing me up! You don’t want to be humiliated in front of a crowd, do you? Now, put ’em up! I’ll smack you around until you can’t even see the wall!”

“Whoa, calm down,” Spike urged. “There’s no need to get violent. We didn’t know you were working on the case. We were trying to—”

“I don’t care what you were trying to do!” I screamed, hopping up and down impatiently.

"You just said you wanted to know why—" Spot started.

I smacked his nose again. *For goodness' sake, you'd think these boneheads could take a hint! But I guess that's why they call them "boneheads"—all bone, no brain.*

"With respect," Specks cut in, plopping down onto his behind, "we are the security dogs of this shelter. The problem of No-Slack Jack's ghost is ours to take care of, and *solely* ours."

"If you knew what *respect* meant, you would back off and leave the investigation to the professional, aka *me*, aka the dog who's going to box you through the wall if you don't line up in an orderly fashion and scuttle your little behinds out of here this instant!" I yapped, throwing my front paws in the air. *Gee, these bozos really don't know how to follow orders, do they?*

"Can I say something?" Mocha wondered aloud.

I stuck my nose in the air. "Yes, of course. *After* these dopes have marched their dopey bottoms out of this cage! March, march, march! Shoo!" I flapped my paws again.

"Um... *no*," Spike said rudely, squaring his shoulders. "This is *our* shelter, *our* problem, *our* investigation. Now, with no respect whatsoever, I order *you* to leave."

Ugh! The nerve!

I puffed out my chest. "Oh? Are we going there? Would you like me to model you after a genuine Picasso painting? And those were 'p' words, by the way. Can I hear a round of applause?"

All three Labradors—along with Mocha—blinked blankly ("b" words!).

"You know what? Never mind," I spat at the boneheads, turning to Mocha. "I shall simply conduct my interrogation as if you three were not here, and when you get bored, you may leave." I cleared my royal throat, sat down, and began. "Mocha, can you pretty please tell me where you were at the time of the ghost's appearance?"

Mocha shrugged. "Sure. I was back here, getting a bite of supper, when that creepy ghoul started shouting. Is that it?"

"Not entirely," I responded.

"Please stop," Spot requested politely.

I rolled my eyes at him. It was a little too late for those lame-brained Labs ("l" words!) to play the manners card.

"Please leave," I returned snottily. Since Spot had decided to play the manners card anyway, I answered with the only reasonable defense—the snooty card.

Suddenly, before I could get any more information out of Mocha, I heard a loud, booming, almost panicked yap from down the hall. It kept going until it grew from a yap to a bark, from a bark to a roar, from a roar to a thunderous blast.

But by that time, I was already racing down the aisle, with Spot, Spike, and Specks right behind me. *No Labrador is going to beat me to the scene of suspicion this time!*

My eyes went wide as I neared said scene. For, if I was not mistaken, the explosion-like *woof*ing sounds were coming from Rex's cage!

CHAPTER NINE (IX, *Nueve*)

A Pricking Prank

Sure enough, though those Labs gave the race everything they had, Luna, Puppy Detective, arrived at Rex's cage first. In case any of you didn't get what I just said...I got there *first*! Hooray! Everybody stand up and clap and spin in a circle and throw your hands into the air and shout for joy! Luna, Puppy Detective, beat out the boneheaded boneheads! Whoo-hoo!

Now, it is my pleasure to present in writing what I snootily yet heroically did next.

My chin held high, my back as straight as my somewhat crooked spine would allow, my tail waving out behind me like a flag of victory, I rushed into Rex's cage, despite the fact that there was a Doberman in there. Pretty brave, huh? Yeah, I think so, too.

Then I stopped, my eyes going wide as they began to water. My paws were being pricked by an unknown enemy! I hopped around frantically, my eyes flooding with moisture that came as a result of my pain, my flag of victory whipping back and forth in desperation, my mouth opening to let out a cry of anguish.

Pins! Someone had put pins on the floor of Rex's cage!

Prancing about like a barefoot human on a frozen river, I spun in a few circles, collided with the wall, tumbled backward, felt the pins stick my queenly back, rolled onto my paws, felt the pins stick my queenly toes, jumped high into the air, and came right back down on the…pins! *Ouch-ouch-ouch! Someone is going to pay for this! I'll sue for the horrible handicapping of my queenly toes!*

Spot, Spike, and Specks all screeched to hurried stops at the entrance to Rex's cage. "Whoa!" exclaimed Spot. "There are *pins* in there!"

Wow, aren't you observant?

"Hold on, Luna!" called Spike. "I'll get you out!"

"You're not worthy to say my name!" I shot back, still prancing. To a human, it would've looked like I was hopping up and down, picking my legs up quite elegantly, and then setting them back down, only to hurriedly lift them up again. A human would think I was dancing or doing something ridiculous like that. But then again, a human is a human. There's no predicting the sheer vastness of their incomprehension. Trust me.

It was at that moment Rex rocketed out of the cage, speeding right past me, pins stuck to the bottom of his paws. He landed in the hallway outside, roaring like a lion with a toothache, until he finally shook all the pins free. Ironically, that was around the time Creeper and Leia arrived on the scene, with pretty much the whole shelter right behind them. *What took them so long?*

"Mommy!" called Leia cheerfully. "Wow! I didn't know you could clog that well!"

"I'm not *clogging*!" I snarled, still prancing on my seriously smarting ("s" words!) royal paws. "Leia, I'm not even *dancing*! There are *pins* on the floor in here!"

"Then why did you go in there?" Leia wanted to know.

"I'll get you out," good old Creeper volunteered, moving forward.

Well, it's about time someone tries to help me!

I struggled to pitter-patter over to the edge of the cage, but found it nearly impossible, as walking and hopping directionally was not desirable to my nearly ruined toes. Straining, I caught a glimpse of my kitten son's expression and knew that he was prepared to fling himself onto the pins and drag me out of there. But someone leapt into the cage before he could.

Cat-Eyes, her green eyes blazing, caught the scruff of my neck and started to haul me quite roughly out of the cage.

"Egh! Stop it!" I snarled. "You're making my neck hurt! Ouch, ouch, ouch!"

She ignored me. *She ignored me!* SHE. IGNORED. ME!

Well, I never!

"Luna!" Creeper was at Cat-Eyes' side the instant she left the cage. My son helped tug me out of the pin-filled trap and onto the soothing, smooth concrete. He leaned down and began carefully plucking out the pins that still clung insistently to me.

"Who did that? I demand to know!" I shouted at the top of my lungs. "I am Luna, Puppy Detective, and I demand some information! Right now! Pronto! This moment!"

"You're *welcome,*" Cat-Eyes said in annoyance.

I stuck my tongue out at her. "Hush up, furball. You only rescued—er, *removed me*—from there because you didn't want to hear my screaming—er, *stupendous shouts of alarm.* Isn't that right?"

Cat-Eyes flicked her tail and licked her bratty whiskers. "Well, what other reason would there be for me risking my good paws? Why I should trick the latch on my cage's door, stick my neck out for you, and not even receive so much as a thank you is beyond me!

"And anyway, I value my keen ears more than I value my toes." She held up one front paw and wiggled it for emphasis, then twitched her ears. "My hearing is better than any old dog's. I can hear everything that goes on in this shelter. If you're looking for information, *Luna,* I'm the one to talk to."

Shoving my queenly nose in her face, I seethed, "I don't need help from you, cat." I then pivoted and yelled loudly, "And, for the record, I don't need help from Labradors, either!"

"Well, that's fine. We don't need help from you," Specks returned sharply.

I squared my shoulders. "What was that? I can't hear you over the sounds of the thousands of little Luna kid fans booing you and your boneheaded brothers."

"Luna, are you all right?" Creeper cut in just before I could slice and dice Specks.

I turned to Creeps and whispered, "I'm fine. But I have some new suspicions to discuss with you. Leia, Creeper, follow me." I turned and started for our cage, shoving through the crowd.

Singing a song about dandelions and space shuttles, Leia followed, her tail wagging back and forth all the way. As for Rex...Well, he stood stiff, watching us go, his eyes narrowed, his paws speckled with small drops of blood. I didn't know it yet, but Rex was fixing to surprise me by acting on a few suspicions of his own.

CHAPTER TEN (X, *Diez*)

Determination and Speculation

"Here's what I'm thinking," I whispered as Creeper, Leia, and I huddled together in the semi-privacy of our cage. The door had been closed and securely latched, seeing as Creeper assured me that he could easily spring us from the cage. We had arranged the newspapers against the door, tucking them into every corner and empty space until we were almost completely shrouded in darkness.

Outside, I could hear three young pups playing Wag! You're It! and two dogs wrestling over a bowl of kibble. The noises of Spot, Spike, and Specks speaking quietly also wafted through the air like a disgusting aroma, but I ignored them for the time being. Whatever investigation those loser Labs were planning on launching, I could easily outdo it with my awesomely awesome and queenly detective skills.

In addition, my ears told me that some dogs and many cats had settled into their cages to catch some shut-eye, while Rex paced restlessly around outside his pin-filled space. The unpleasant words he was uttering seemed to be describing how much he disliked me, and were I to quote exactly what he said, I'm sure your parents would not be pleased. I'm just going to reveal this: That dope was insulting Luna, Puppy Detective, claiming that I had no skills whatsoever in detective work! Can you believe that? *Eh, what a bozo.*

"I suspect Cat-Eyes has a part in this," I declared at last, holding up one paw in a very professor-like manner.

"But, Mommy," Leia objected, "Cat-Eyes has brown fur with black stripes. She doesn't have nearly enough black fur to produce that big clump left at the crime scene."

"Yes," Creeper agreed. "If the clump belonged to Cat-Eyes, wouldn't there have been brown fur mixed in with the black?"

I waved my paw dismissively. "Minor concerns, Creeper, minor concerns. But now, on to the large suspicions!" I lowered my voice so anybody that might be eavesdropping on our puppy powwow ("p" words!) wouldn't be able to hear me. "Cat-Eyes just stated that she *can* get out of her cage, right? What I'm thinking is, she begged to be let out when we first arrived just to make us think she *couldn't* get out by herself. Then, when those loser Labs wouldn't let her out, she sprung herself from the cage and employed her sneaky cat skills to put on the show of No-Slack Jack's ghost!"

"Wait," Creeper cut in. I made a mental note to school him on the no-interrupting rule—the one parents school their kids on—at a later date. "Before we start making assumptions, we have to determine for certain *who* the ghost is."

"That's easy," Leia piped up. "No-Flapjacks!" She scrunched up one eye. "I wonder if he's allergic to flapjacks."

I rolled my eyes, not even bothering to correct my silly sidekick. "Creeper means *what* the ghost is, Leia."

Leia put on her Thinking Face. "A ghost?" she tried, confused.

Huffing, I turned to Creeper. "The question that immediately pops into my mind is—what is the ghost made of?"

"Ectoplasm?" Leia guessed.

"*No,*" I growled. "I mean, *what is the*...? Never mind! The point is, someone is trying to make everyone in this shelter think there's a ghost, and there really isn't. Now, let's do a bit of brainstorming here. If I was someone trying to make everyone in this shelter think there's a ghost, and there really isn't, what would I use to create it? Would I dress up? Well, if I'm Cat-Eyes, I'm too catlike to be the ghost of a dog. From the size of the ghost, I'd bet No-Slack Jack was a big dog, too. So that puts Cat-Eyes dressing up out of the question."

"Ooh! Ooh! I know! Little Red Riding Hood was going to get attacked by the Big Bad Wolf, so she dressed up in ectoplasm to disguise herself as the ghost of a dog called No-Turning-Back Jack!" Leia burst out.

"First of all, it's *No-Slack Jack,* Leia, and second of all, this has *nothing* to do with Little Red Riding Hood and ectoplasm!" I exploded.

"Guess what?" Leia asked out of nowhere. "I was guarding the newspaper, and Darling came back and we chatted. We chatted about a lot of things, and I told her about the pretty black fur we found. She said it was cool that we picked up a clue. She said the fur looks a lot like Spot's."

"*You told Darling about the...?*" I started, but then trailed off, my eyes widening. "Wait, Leia. What did you just say?"

Leia grinned goofily ("g" words!) and repeated verbatim, "Guess what? I was guarding the newspaper, and Darling came back and we chatted. We chatted about a lot of things, and I told her—"

"Darling said the fur looks like Spot's?" I interrupted, giving a little hop, which really hurt my queenly toes, even though they weren't on pins anymore. "That loser Lab! I knew he had something to do with this. He's always annoying me with that snotty little voice of his and..." I paused, staring intently at Creeper, who appeared to be deep in thought. "Creeps, something on your mind?"

"I was just thinking," Creeper began, "about the ghost's eyes and its red teeth. If it was someone dressed up, how did they get glowing eyes and red teeth?"

"We've just been over this. If Cat-Eyes is behind the whole thing, she wouldn't dress up." I stopped as a sudden thought struck me. "Perhaps she has an accomplice!"

"Spot?" Leia spoke up, reading my mind. Her eyes grew ten times the size they should've been, and she broke down sobbing. "Spot's a nice doggy! He wouldn't commit a crime like that!"

"What about Rex?" I went on. "He is always bothering dogs. Maybe this is his latest prank to scare the current residents of this shelter."

"Rex?" Leia demanded, still in tears. Now she began ruthlessly pounding the floor of the cage in her growing shock and sorrow. "*NOT REX*, Mommy! Rex is my buddy! He's my nice friendy-wendy!"

"First of all, Rex is *not* your buddy, and he's not a nice...a nice...*whatever* you just said he was," I snapped.

"But why would Rex put pins on the floor of his own cage?" Creeper wondered aloud. "It doesn't make sense."

"Maybe he was trying to make us suspect someone else," I proposed. "And by saving me, Cat-Eyes was trying to divert suspicion from herself, and by investigating and therefore attempting to help me solve the mystery, Spot was trying to divert suspicion from himself."

"So we've narrowed it down to three basic suspects," Creeper summarized. "Cat-Eyes, Rex, and Spot."

"But the other Labs tried to help, too," Leia piped up.

I patted my daughter sympathetically on the head. Sometimes Leia doesn't catch on to concepts as quickly as I do. In fact, she hardly *ever* does.

"Leia, Leia, Leia," I said, clicking my tongue and shaking my head. "We only found *Spot*'s fur on the crime scene. Granted, Spike and Specks are annoying. They are, for the time being, *possible suspects*, which means we don't have enough proof yet that they're involved. We do, however, have hard-core evidence to support the fact that three definite suspects—Cat-Eyes, Rex, and Spot—were trying to look innocent."

"What about Buster?" Leia asked suddenly.

I was taken aback. *Wow, Leia really* does *pay attention when I'm making my deductions! I had no idea! I'll have to promote her from my sidekick to... Well, I'll probably just commend her for being a good sidekick. That sounds good to me.*

"He lied," Creeper agreed with Leia. "We know he wasn't trying to jimmy the side door when the ghost appeared."

"Perhaps he is in on this, too," I speculated, one paw to my chin in deep contemplation. I looked up.

"Maybe he's in clawhoots with Cat-Eyes!" Don't you love the play on the word "cahoots" I used there? "*Claw*hoots"? As in dogs and cats? Claws? Yes? No? Never mind. On with the story.

"How many crooks are we talking about?" Creeper asked, hurrying to calculate sums in his head.

"Four. Possibly more," I supplied. Prissily, I then straightened. "But I have a theory." Lowering my voice because I was still suspicious of unwanted listeners, I muttered to Leia and Creeper, "I think we might be dealing with a band of street animals because of the suspects' numbers."

"OH, NO!" Leia wailed for the whole shelter—eavesdropping or not—to hear. "NOT STREET ANIMALS! OH, MOMMY!" She scrunched up one eye, scratching at a flea in quite a clueless manner. "What does that have to do with anything?"

"*Shh,* Leia," I hissed, glancing around me wildly. Nobody seemed terribly disturbed by Leia. The puppies playing Wag! You're It! paused, but then went on like nothing had happened. The two wrestling dogs didn't stop at all. The sleeping animals only stirred, then started snoring ("s" words!). Spot, Spike, and Specks left to go check on their master, the security guard. *Phew. That was close.*

"You think a band of street animals smuggled themselves into this shelter one at a time to cause chaos and drama?" Creeper asked.

"Yes, that's exactly what I'm saying." That was, at the moment, the only reason I could see for four animals to be working together on a crime in a place where nobody typically commits crimes.

Considering this, Creeper lifted his paw to his chin as well. "Why would they want to do that?"

"Perhaps the story of No-Slack Jack holds some answers," I proposed. "Cat-Eyes seems to know about the legend of the old shelter dog. Maybe we can question her!"

"When?" Creeper demanded. "The sun is coming up. The Labs will be leaving soon, and we'll all have to be back in our cages. It's almost opening time."

I sighed, staring down at the floor thoughtfully. "Well, all we need is a well-structured plan, and we can be out during the day without the humans noticing. Humans aren't in here all the time, after all."

"But someone will come in here to fix the cages Rex busted," Creeper pointed out. "We have to put the case on pause or risk being locked up more securely. We can't put this whole investigation in jeopardy. It would be smarter to postpone it until closing time."

I huffed again. "Fine, fine. Creeps, get that newspaper looking back to normal. We're going undercover for the day as cute, innocent little Shih Tzu dogs! Oh, and also a cute, innocent little *cat.* We'll lay low, and then we'll strike tonight, launching my brilliant plan to solve the case once and for all!"

"Then we eat!" Leia cheered, hopping up and down. "Eat! Eat! Eat!"

"Yes, Leia," I mumbled grumpily. "Then we can eat."

CHAPTER ELEVEN (XI, *Once*)

Laying Low/Return of the Ghost

Waiting all day made me miserable. I alternated between sitting and pacing, my nails clicking impatiently as I moved about my cage, with Darling occasionally commenting on how unwell I looked, Creeper constantly shifting in his cage above me, and Leia napping in the corner.

A few minutes after our puppy powwow, Creeper had returned to his cage, and Darling had come to ours, just when Leia and I had finished rearranging the newspaper on the floor. Of course, I didn't reveal anything of what was said at the powwow to Darling, because I don't like the idea of sharing my suspicions with anyone except those I *know* I can trust. Do I know I can trust Leia? No. But she's pretty much with me twenty-four/seven, so trustworthy or not, she's in on all my secrets.

It was almost opening time when I got fed up and started slamming my queenly head against the wall. However, a fit of hysterics and a broken skull wouldn't help me, so after a friendly reminder of this fact from Darling, I backed up and sat on my haunches, thinking hard. At that moment, Rex bounded over, sticking his nose up to the chain-link on the front of my cage.

"I'll chew you up, runt, if you ever do that again," he barked.

I tilted my head in confusion. "Do *what* again?"

"Don't play silly, prissy dog. You planted those pins on the floor of my cage to make me look like a sissy. Then you ran in there to make yourself look innocent. Well, you'd better watch out. There's no telling what'll happen to you when the humans aren't watching," snarled Rex, licking his lips. "I've been thinking about it. And I've been thinking about *you.*" He leaned in closer, and his nose pressed the chain-link forward, which created a small dent in the door.

A puddle of yellow formed underneath me. But it wasn't because I was scared, mind you—I was just used to being let outside first thing in the morning to *relieve myself,* that's all. Rex just *happened* to be standing there when I lost control and *relieved myself.* End of story.

"This is your warning," Rex continued. To my right, I heard Leia let out a long, loud snore. She plopped her chubby paws over her nose and wagged her tail, dreaming of doughnuts and ice cream shops.

Gee, she's a big help.

"W-warning?" I stammered (heroically, I might add—it takes a great hero to act humble in the presence of a dope such as Rex).

"If you ever come near me or my cage again, I'll kill you, prissy dog," Rex threatened. "And don't take that lightly," he added, as if I would've considered the idea that he was joking. "I've brought down plenty of dogs in the past, and they were a lot bigger and tougher than you. Think twice next time before you do *anything* to old Rex." Laughing wickedly, Rex wheeled and trotted to a vacant cage, hopping into it and closing the door behind him.

I stood, frozen, for a few seconds. Then I squinted one eye. *Rex thinks I put pins on the floor of his cage! That's not fair. He doesn't have any proof. None whatsoever! How can he accuse me, Luna, Puppy Detective, of such a crime? He can't, and I ought to tell him that! Then again, he* did *tell me that if I came near him, he would choose a course of violent actions that would most likely result in my death.*

I sighed and turned, plopping down onto my bottom—and also onto the urine-soaked newspaper. *Ew!* I scooted off the wet spot, planting myself instead in the corner opposite Leia's. Glancing at me, Darling settled onto a dry area of the newspaper to get some sleep, too. That meant I was sitting there with no company but my thoughts, which swam at the speed of fish fleeing an ocean predator.

The day dragged by slowly, as I previously mentioned. Slower than an elephant dragging the Empire State Building. Slower than a slug in a tar pit. Slower than slow itself!

I slept. I thought. I slept some more. And still the day stretched on, tormenting me with each passing millisecond. On top of that, nothing much really happened. A tall, overall-clad handyman stopped by to repair the two broken cages. As far as adopters went, there was only one girl who arrived and left within five minutes, selecting a cat I wasn't familiar with to take home. A few shelter volunteers came and went. I was taken out of my cage for a small walk in the outdoor run, but after recognizing my snooty, stubborn nature, the human who was doing the walking quickly took me back inside and returned me to my cage. So I went back to thinking.

Basically, I was trying to gather my thoughts and put all the puzzle pieces of this mystery into place. Cat-Eyes, Rex, Spot, and Buster were in league, I was sure. They had all worked together to create the ghost hoax, I was sure. They were crooked crooks working to accomplish something (but I didn't know what), I was sure. What I *wasn't* sure of was the motive, the means...

Are they all street animals or not? Why are they doing all this? Why would three totally different dogs work with a cat? What do they stand to gain, anyway?

Sitting in silence in the middle of a cage gave me plenty of time to reflect on everything. Where did I end up? Back at square one—Cat-Eyes, Rex, Spot, and Buster were in league. Where did I go from there?

To sleep. That's where I went immediately.

I awoke to the sound of a clock *gong-gong-gong-gong*ing. *Hmmm. Four* gong*s. Four o'clock! Closing time!*

I leapt to my paws and started shaking Leia wildly. "Leia, Leia, wake up!" I yapped. "We have an investigation to conduct!"

"Cool," piped up Darling. "Have you guys found anything out?"

I turned my nose up at her. "That's privileged information."

The spotted Dalmatian's ears sagged, and she hung her head. Clearly Darling was hurt by the fact that I didn't trust her enough to share the latest developments in the No-Slack Jack case with her. "Oh," she mumbled glumly.

I scooted in front of her, angling my head so I could meet her eyes. "Hey, cheer up. I just don't have everything *organized* yet, that's all. I'll tell you when I've figured out the case, okay?"

Darling perked up and thumped her tail. "Okay."

Behind me, I heard the loud, overly exaggerated yawn of my sidekick as her heavy eyelids squinted open. She smacked her lips and rolled over, playing with her chub. Then, yawning again, she rolled onto her pudgy paws and plodded over to where I stood. "Morning, Mommy," Leia greeted, her eyes still squinted in a sleepy manner.

"It's not *morning*, Leia," I pointed out flatly.

"It isn't? Oh, wow! Days are just going by faster and faster. Well, then I guess I can go back to sleep." Happily, Leia waddled to the far end of the cage, tucked her paws underneath her, and started to lower her head.

"*No*, Leia," I hissed.

Leia jumped up. "What? Who? What happened?"

"Leia, *we have an investigation to conduct*," I repeated in annoyance.

Closing her eyes, Leia twitched her whiskers. "But you said it wasn't morning," she drawled carelessly.

"Leia, you slept practically *all* day. Time to *get up*," I growled. It took me a few seconds to realize how backward my words sounded.

Leia smacked her lips again and started to snore.

Okay, fine. I don't really need Leia for my sleuthing tonight, anyway.

Huffing, I made my way to the front of the cage and stared out of the chain-link, willing those loser Labs to appear and release me. *Wait! I don't want those loser Labs releasing me! What horrid damage that would cause to my dignity! No! I have a better idea!*

"Creeps!" I called upward.

"What's up?" Creeper called back from the cage he was in, which was situated on top of mine.

"Flip your latch and come get me out," I ordered, sticking my chin in the air royally and curling my queenly Shih Tzu tail. I would've opened the door myself, little Luna kid fans, but you see, God made cats and dogs differently; otherwise, we'd be living in a world full of cats and dogs that were the same, and that concept is too alien for me to discuss right now.

Okay, let's talk a little bit about anatomy. Dogs were made by God to be nimble, quick, yet somewhat stockier and less flexible than cats. Cats, on the other hand, were created to be agile and have ridiculously bendable abilities. Therefore, only a cat could've reached through the chain-link, twisted its arm, and flipped the latch. There we go. Your parents should write me a thank-you note for throwing some quality education into my book, and they better send some sort of savory snack with it (lots of "s" words!).

A few seconds after I had voiced my request, Creeper's door swung open, and he landed in the hallway in front of my door, reaching out and easily popping the latch. I shot out like a lightning bolt the instant I was able, whirling to see if Leia was following. *Nope. She's still asleep. Oh, well.* However, I did notice that someone else had left the cage besides me—Darling. She positioned herself next to Creeper and me, grinning. "I'm going to go visit with Benson," Darling told us, wagging her tail and panting. "I'll let him out of his cage."

I nodded. "Good for you. Now, Creeps, come on." I turned and trotted down the hall with Creeper, and when Darling went to let Benson out, I quickly doubled back with my kitten son and ended up standing before Cat-Eyes' cage. It's all part of my trick in case someone's watching me, you see. A queenly Shih Tzu sleuth has to be unpredictable in her maneuvers; otherwise, all her suspicions would be out for the whole world to see.

"Oh, lookie who it is," muttered Cat-Eyes in annoyance.

Nearby, I heard a dog stir in its cage. I lowered my voice to a whisper so nobody could hear and asked, "So, kitty-kitty, what do *you* know of the story of No-Slack Jack?"

Cat-Eyes flicked her tail, blinking at me innocently. "Oh, and *why* would you want to know that, Loony?"

"It's *Luna,*" I corrected. What was up with everyone mispronouncing my name? First Buster and now Cat-Eyes! I had a feeling, though, that Cat-Eyes was doing it now just to get on my nerves. And of all the names she could've used—*Loony*! I am not the slightest bit loony, and the whole world knows it! That selfish, annoying, no-good…

"What are you doing?" asked a sudden voice from behind me.

I whirled around and came nose-to-nose with one of my top suspects—Spot the Labrador! Behind him stood Spike and Specks, wearing their security vests. They apparently had arrived in the hallway right when I was about to heroically interrogate Cat-Eyes. *What sneaks!*

Then I squinted, realizing that Spot wasn't wearing his vest. *Hmmm. I wonder what happened to it…*

"We are here conducting business that you are not to interrupt," Creeper spat sharply, and even I jumped in surprise. Generally, Creeper's only snotty to irritating cats like Pip.

"What happened to your vest?" I asked Spot outright. I'm not one to mess around when it comes to crooked crooks, and Spot struck me as the crooked crook type.

"Lost it," mumbled Spot, sounding embarrassed as he stared at the floor. He nervously traced a line across the concrete with one paw.

"Emma," Spike filled in quickly for Spot, "our owner's four-year-old daughter."

"You'd think she'd have enough to play with, what with all of her toys and crafts and such," Specks spoke up.

"She stole my vest," Spot grumbled. "I don't know where she put it."

I straightened. "Well, I hereby give your brothers leave to go and look for your vest. You, on the other hand, I have some questions for."

Spike's eyes widened. "*You're* giving *us* permission to leave the shelter that *we* protect?"

"No. I'm *ordering* you to leave this shelter, which you are doing a *horrible* job of protecting, seeing as this ghost character is terrorizing the place," I said shortly, puffing out my queenly chest.

"That's right!" yelled a familiar voice that sounded from all directions.

I jumped and, together with Creeper, craned my neck toward the sound.

"No animal leaves this shelter! I *must* have my revenge!" screamed the ghoulish voice as a figure soared high above our heads.

I gulped. The ghost of No-Slack Jack was back!

CHAPTER TWELVE (XII, *Doce*)

Leia Talks Somewhat Sensible Nonsense

"Ah!" shrieked Mocha from nearby. "It's the ghost!"

"Woof! Woof!" thundered Rex.

"Save me, save me!" squealed a very high-pitched voice from Buster's cage.

Ooh! What a sissy!

"Creeps!" I shouted, but Creeper was already scaling the cages, preparing for a hard-core attack on the ghoulish ghoul.

"Stop that ghost!" commanded Spike, gesturing wildly at No-Slack Jack.

"Stop!" Specks tried lamely.

Spot growled and leapt into the air, snapping for one of the ghost's mummified paws. He missed, spiraling back down and landing on his snotty nose. *Ha. Serves him right.*

In a very queenly fashion, I whirled and scurried back to my cage. "Leia!" I snarled to my sleeping sidekick ("s" words!). "Front and center! Red alert! There is a ghost flying around!"

"You will *never* leave this shelter!" the ghost screeched, waving its paws and flashing its red teeth. "Mark my words!"

With that, it soared up so high that it cleared the row of cages again, but this time Creeper got to the top, too. The instant he did, though, he came tumbling back down, his paws flailing wildly. Eyes widening, I dashed forward and caught Creeps by the scruff of his neck.

"Are you okay?" I asked.

Creeper nodded. "I think so. The ghost swung around and knocked me off at the last second."

I grinned. "So it's *not* a ghost. It's solid!"

"Puppies can't eat solid food when they're first born," Leia told me, stretching and looking around her. "Gee, what are my Lab friends looking so worried about?"

"After him!" shouted Specks frantically, referring to the ghost.

"No use," grumbled Spike. "Those cages' backs meet the wall. He must've floated right through it."

"Ahem!" I waved my paw in Spike's face. "I *believe* I just *said* that the ghost is not a ghost because he is solid! How then, bozo, can you propose the ridiculous possibility of him phasing through the wall?"

"Because he's a *ghost*," said all three Labs at the same time.

"There is no such thing as a *ghost*," I snarled, blinking and giving the ground a small yet fancy smack for emphasis.

"We know *that*," Spot told me, rolling his eyes. "What we mean is that, whatever that thing is, it can probably phase through walls."

"Yeah, and *that* makes a lot of sense." I turned to Creeper. "You head down to Buster's cage and ask him about that lock lie. I've got some matters to discuss with these boneheads."

"We're right here, you know," Specks cut in.

I nodded. "I know, bonehead. Now, Creeper, go, go, go!"

Creeper turned, zooming off for the Tibetan Mastiff's cage. Prissily, I pivoted, fixing my queenly gaze on the three Labrador punks.

"I'm going to need a fur sample from Spot," I informed them. "I must compare it with a bit of significant evidence I have unearthed at the original scene of the crime. Now, should any of you wish to question me, I shall remove every last ounce of fur from your sorry hides. Any questions?"

"Are you nuts?" Spike demanded.

I huffed. "I really had hoped I wouldn't have to pluck you like a chicken, Spike. However, it is clear that you are suffering from all-around meanness, so I must correct you. Leia, you don't happen to have a pair of tweezers handy, do you?"

Leia, who had turned to get a drink of water, now waddled out of the cage and yawned. "Well, I could go up to the top of the cages and look for some there," Leia proposed.

"Hey, guys," Darling said suddenly, trotting up with Benson beside her. "Whatcha doing?"

I ignored her, realizing what Leia had just said. "Leia, you've been up *on top* of the cages?"

"Only once," Leia admitted quickly. She grinned. "Rex and I were playing Toss the Squeaky Toy. He accidentally tossed it way, way up onto the cage tops. So he let me climb up on his back and get up there. And boy, did I have a hard time finding it! Do you know how much stuff is up there, Mommy? There isn't even room for dust!"

"Leia, what all is up there?" I asked, not even caring that a bunch of dorky bozos were listening, aka Spike, Specks, and Spot, plus Benson and Darling (who weren't really dorky bozos, but who I didn't want hearing any privileged testimony if I could avoid it).

"Oh, I don't remember, Mommy," Leia chirped.

I smacked my forehead. "Leia, how come you can never remember *anything* vital to our cases?" She licked her lips and grinned, apparently proud of her inability to recall instances. In my last mystery, *Luna: Puppy Detective #1: Catnapped!*, Leia had forgotten something so important that it could've cost me the whole case. Blessedly, though, it *didn't* cost me the whole case, so I had forgiven her. But here she was again, forgetting something that probably *would* cost me the whole case!

Then another thought struck me: *Leia said she was playing Toss the Squeaky Toy with Rex! When did she do this?*

"Leia, *when* were you playing toss?" I asked, my heart quickening in eagerness.

"Oh, while you were sleeping this morning, Mommy," Leia supplied happily, thumping her tail.

I wrinkled my royal brow. "How did you get out?"

Leia grinned and thumped her tail some more. "The door was open."

I was taken aback. "Leia, you were dreaming. There's no way the door to our cage was open in the daytime when people could've easily come in and seen you out of it. Did Creeper open the door?"

I didn't think Creeper would do a thing like that. Still, Leia can be quite persuasive to her "little bro," as she calls him.

"I can't remember, Mommy."

"Of course you can't." I turned to the Labs. "What are you sticking around for? Beat it."

"Hold on," Spot objected. "This could be a crucial development in the case!"

"Yes. But this is *my* case, not yours, so get off my case," I growled, "or I'll smack you in the nose again, and this time, it'll de-nose you."

"De-nose?" Spike whispered to Specks, who shrugged.

"Now, I'd like to continue my sleuthing in *private,* if you don't mind. So if you won't leave, I shall be forced to relocate myself to a more secure area of the premises."

"An obscure Maria of the promises?" Leia asked, confused.

I indicated Leia fiercely with my paw. "Yes, yes, what she said!" Realizing Leia had said it *wrong*, I quickly amended, "Well, no, *not* what she said, but... The point is that you must leave!"

"Okay, okay, fine. We'll probably get better information elsewhere, anyway," snorted Spike. He whirled and sashayed away smugly.

"Spike, come on. Be nice," implored Spot, turning to follow his brother. With a roll of his eyes, Specks trailed Spike and Spot.

"Luna, why don't you want their help?" Benson asked. "They're just trying to aid you in solving the case."

"They are trying to solve the case for me," I corrected, bopping him on his Beagle nose. "Nobody, repeat *nobody*, tries to beat out Luna, Puppy Detective, while she is unraveling a mystery! NOBODY! Got that?"

Benson nodded hurriedly. "Yup. Got it. I suppose Darling and I should go then?"

I blinked. "Well, if you don't mind."

"Sure thing." Darling turned and, with Benson right on her heels, trotted away.

"Your friends are so nice," cooed Leia, plopping down on her bottom and watching her chub jiggle.

"Now, Leia," I whispered, dropping down beside my daughter, "I want you to tell me all that you did when you were out with Rex."

"Ooh! Ooh! We played Toss the Squeaky Toy!"

I nodded. "Yes, of course. But what else?"

Leia opened her mouth, but just then, a snarling sound came from the direction of Buster's cage.

Creeper!

Turning, I raced off with Leia right behind me for the shadowy suspect's confined space.

CHAPTER THIRTEEN (XIII, *Trece*)

Busting Buster

The instant I jumped into Buster's open cage, I analyzed the situation. Buster was tumbling around, snapping and snarling at Creeper. What does a queenly Shih Tzu detective such as myself do when her adoptive kitten son is in danger?

You guessed it. I pounced right into the fray.

"Go, Mommy!" Leia cheered, throwing her paws in the air. "Go, Mommy! Give me an M! Give me an O! Give me an M! Give me a double E! Mommy!"

Egh. I'll have to work with Leia on her spelling later.

I bit Buster's ear and felt myself being rolled around. Frantically, I swatted Buster in the right eye. He let out a high-pitched yelp as Creeper sank his claws deep into the Tibetan Mastiff's shoulder.

"Creeps," I said through a mouthful of ear, "hurry up! We have to get him under—"

Buster jerked violently to the side, cutting me off.

"Control!" Creeper finished for me. He fastened his jaws on the side of Buster's neck.

"Get offa me!" yelled Buster, managing to scramble to his paws and spin in a circle. This flung me off, and I went flying out of control through midair, colliding with Leia.

I knocked her flat on her back and found myself on top of her, pinning her there. Leia grinned up at me. "Hi, Mommy. Did you tag me? Am I it now?"

Ignoring her, I bounced off and royally inserted myself back into the center of the melee, this time clamping my teeth shut on the edge of Buster's tail.

He let out a loud, humiliating, puppy-like squeal, and then spun around again, flapping his tail violently back and forth in an attempt to throw me off once more. This time, I held fast, my front paws also fastened around the brute's tail.

Meanwhile, Creeper had managed to get onto Buster's left shoulder blade and crawl up along his neck. In triumph, my kitten son now had Buster's muzzle between his two clawed front paws. "That's a good doggy," Creeper crooned as Buster whipped his head back and forth. "Slow down there, boy. Sit. Lie down. Roll over."

"AAAARGH!" Buster screamed, turning and slamming Creeper against a wall.

"Go, little bro! Go, little bro!" chanted Leia, spinning in a circle and clapping her paws. "Whoo-hoo!"

"Leia! Leia!" I called, suddenly inspired. "There's a hamburger on Buster's head!" Buster's tail swept out, plunking me onto the floor. I held on tighter as I was whisked back into the air.

"A big ol' hambugger?" Leia asked excitedly, thumping her tail. She grinned. "Oh, boy!"

With that, Leia flew forward, landing right on top of Buster's head. Her weight shoved his nose onto the ground, and he squealed quite noisily, ceasing his struggles.

"Victory!" Creeper declared, sliding off Buster's snout.

"Sorry, sir," Leia said to Buster, lifting up one paw so she could look into his right eye. "I didn't mean to make your head go *thump*." Then she perked up, asking almost sheepishly, "Could you direct me to the big ol' hambugger?"

Shaking head to paws from the bone-jarring fight I had just endured, I stumbled over to Creeper, then turned to Buster and grinned. "Looks like we just busted you, Buster," I taunted. Buster growled, trying to lift his head. However, Leia's overwhelming weight was too much, and he sank back down. I began prancing back and forth in front of the Tibetan Mastiff bozo, now fully confident that I had Buster all figured out. "I've been thinking, Buster, about how you *lied* regarding jimmying the lock when the ghost first appeared."

Buster stopped struggling, his eyes going wide. "How did you know?" he asked, astonished.

"Well, you gave yourself away. The ghost just appeared for a second time since my arrival, correct? I heard you screaming like a blind mouse with its tail cut off," I informed him, my head held high in pride.

"Oh, you mean the three blind mice?" Leia spoke up. "Ooh, that's one of my favorite poems! Just like the one about Simple Simon! *Simple Simon was a pie man—*"

"*Anyway*," I interrupted Leia, huffing as I rolled my eyes, "the point is that Buster is a lying loser who's too much of a chicken to admit that he was scared of a little old ghost."

"Am not," Buster whimpered, sniffling. "I was jimmying the lock."

"No, *we* were jimmying the lock. *You* were hiding in your cage like a scared puppy, whimpering your heart out. But, coward or not, I hereby place you under cage arrest," I announced, raising one paw authoritatively, "until I have this whole No-Slack Jack case figured out."

"Cage arrest?" snarled Buster, forgetting his humiliation and baring his teeth. "What gives ya the authority to do that, Lola, Puggy Incentive?"

"We've been over this. It's *Luna, Puppy Detective*," I corrected, my Shih Tzu tail curling in irritation. *Seriously, what's so hard about my name?* "And I have been appointed to the high position of queen over

Svalbard, the US, and the rest of the world. Any questions?"

"Yeah. Who were ya appointed by?"

I was taken aback. He dared question my dignified lineage? "It is my birthright!" I practically screamed at the bozo.

He wriggled, trying to get out from under Leia to no avail. "Okay, okay, fine, whateva," he snapped. "Just get this…this…this *bowling ball* offa me!"

Leia looked behind her. "Bowling ball? I thought it was a big ol' hambugger, not a bowling ball!"

"Leia, it is pronounced *hamburger,*" I told her for the fifty-five millionth time.

"Okay, basically, you're under cage arrest, so you can either cooperate or suffer the consequences," Creeper summarized at that moment, leaning down so he was at eye level with the Tibetan Mastiff. That sounds really weird, I know—Creeper, a kitten, leaning down to be eye level with a 150-pound Mastiff. Remember, though, little Luna kid fans, Leia was crushing Buster's skull into the ground, and Creeper's head was definitely aboveground, so Creeper had to bend down in order to make eye contact. Okay, nobody has questions anymore? Great! Continuing on…

"What are the consequences, puffball?" Buster demanded, barely able to open his jaw because of the pressure being exerted on his forehead.

I smiled. "Leia, do you know how to clog?"

"Well, I suppose I could try." Leia stood up—still on Buster's head—and started to pick up her paws in a rhythmic fashion.

"Wait! No!" wailed Buster. "I'll stay like a good boy! I promise!"

"That's more like it." I sighed. "Okay, Leia, fun's over. Get off the poor monster."

Leia happily hopped ("h" words!) from Buster's head and landed on her plump paws ("p" words—two alliterations in the same sentence!), smiling at me in an overly friendly manner. "Do you still want to see my clogging, Mommy?" she asked, her tail wagging back and forth. Her whole rear end wagged with it.

"No," I said shortly. Then I turned to Creeper. "Well, let's lock this cage up. Old Buster's been put in his place *and* put under cage arrest. That ought to teach him to mess with Luna, Puppy Detective!"

Though Buster's back legs were extended and his rear end arched high in the air, his chin remained firmly planted on the floor, as if he had forgotten how to lift his head. "Ugh, that dog was *heavy,*" he groaned as he started to strain, attempting to raise his snout. No doubt he had a horrible neck cramp.

"See you, Buster. Remember, if you mess with me or my kitten again, I'll bust you," I jeered. Still rising slowly, Buster glared at me, silently vowing to beat up on me later. That was an empty threat because nobody beats up Luna, Puppy Detective.

Flipping my right ear in a haughty way, I strutted out of the cage, with Creeper at my side and Leia behind me. Once we reached the outside, Buster lunged, but Creeper had already knocked the door shut, which trapped Buster inside.

"Now, we will be conducting periodic checks to make sure you *stay* there," I rattled off in a monotone. "It's mostly to ensure that those loser Labs don't come and let you out. If that were to happen, I would have to contain all four of you. Thank you and good night."

I pivoted, then paused, turning to Creeper. "Do you think I should tell him his Matilda rights?"

"You mean his *Miranda* rights?" Creeper inquired.

I shook my head. "Tomato-tomahtoe. Never mind. Let's go."

CHAPTER FOURTEEN (XIV, *Catorce*)

The Toilet Paper Clue

"All right, this cage is the rendezvous point." I tapped the newspaper on the floor of our cage for emphasis. Huddled together like a football team, Creeper, Leia, and I were prepared to discuss our plan of action. "First of all, I'd like to talk about the case up to this point. I no longer suspect Buster of foul play."

"Buster cheats?" Leia asked, completely mistaking my meaning.

I rolled my eyes. "*No,* Leia. In fact, we have no proof to indicate he breaks rules in any way. We only have proof that he's a wimp. That doesn't mean he's a criminal. Suspicion on Cat-Eyes and Spot has dwindled as well, since Cat-Eyes was in her cage and Spot, along with his brothers, was right by me when the ghost appeared the second time. That leaves only Rex."

Leia raised her paw.

"*Yes*, Leia?"

"Rex and I played Toss the Squeaky Toy this morning."

"*Yes*, I know, Leia."

"He lifted me up onto the top of the cages."

"*Yes*, you've made that very clear, Leia."

"There was toilet paper up there!"

This was a truckload of new information, and it had just rolled over me like I was an oblivious animal crossing the street. (Please do not mistake my meaning, little Luna kid fans. I am alive and well and have *not* been run over by a truck full of new information.)

"Toilet paper?" Creeper asked before I could.

Leia nodded enthusiastically. "Yup. There was lots and lots of toilet paper."

"Anything else?" I questioned eagerly. *Does Leia hold the key to the solution of this mystery?*

But I should've known that Leia couldn't keep her mind on one subject for more than approximately five seconds. She immediately scratched at a flea. "Hmm?"

"*Toilet paper*, Leia. You said there was toilet paper on top of the cages," I yapped, by now trembling with the desire to know what hidden clues Leia had discovered. "Was there anything *else*?"

"Anything else *where*?"

"ON TOP OF THE CAGES!"

"What cages?"

"The cages here in the *shelter*, Leia!"

"What about them?"

"*What was on top of them*?"

"On top of what?"

"LEEEEEEEEEEEEEEEEEEEEEEEEEIA!" I screamed at the top of my lungs, sinking onto my queenly chest and letting my legs spread out. Honestly, having a conversation with Leia is like trying to talk to the floor! You get absolutely nowhere except annoyed when you don't get a satisfactory response! I huffed. "All right, here's the plan: Creeper, I want you to climb up onto those cages and make sense out of Leia's toilet paper mumbo jumbo. I want to know what's up there."

"Yes, ma'am," Creeper said instantly, saluting.

Aw, he's so polite!

"Leia," I continued, "you're coming with me to interrogate Rex."

Leia thumped her tail. “Cool! I’ve never integrated anybody before!”

Ugh, why am I bringing Leia? I quickly reminded myself, however, that Rex liked Leia. In fact, just about *everyone* at the shelter liked Leia. If I had my chubby daughter with me, there was a higher chance of interrogative success. Yes, it should’ve been the other way around. Leia’s goofy presence should’ve triggered distraction from the suspect, not cooperation, and my presence alone should’ve aroused reverence and immediate submission to my inquiries. Why wasn’t it that way? Well, let me put it in a very plain, simple statement, little Luna kid fans: I’m so awesome that sometimes people forget how awesome I am. It’s unfortunate, but it happens quite frequently.

“All right, everybody. Game on.” Creeper turned and sped for the cages opposite ours, grabbing the chain-link with his claws and hopping from one to the next. Cat-Eyes, who still sat inside her cage, let out a little hiss, but Creeper paid her no mind.

“Come on, Leia.” I jogged toward Rex’s cage with her right on my heels.

At that moment, however, I heard an awful roaring sound and then, "GET OUT OF MY CAGE, YOU GOOD-FOR-NOTHING MUTT!"

Both Leia and I froze as Spot the Labrador stumbled out of Rex's cage, whimpering, with one eye squinted, apparently having sustained a slap of the claws across his face. Spot stumbled past us, shedding profusely, with his tail tucked between his legs. As he disappeared into a vacant cage to nurse his wound, I stared down at the floor.

Black fur.

"Identical," I muttered. "Leia, this looks just like the tuft of fur found at the crime scene." I looked up and suddenly realized that Leia wasn't next to me!

CHAPTER FIFTEEN (XV, *Quince*)

A Tight Spot

Eyes wide, I spun around, frantically searching for my daughter. *Oh, where is she? Where is she? Where is she?*

Surely Leia had not turned invisible. I learned that she is not capable of such a feat in *Luna: Puppy Detective #1: Catnapped!* But still…If Leia hadn't turned invisible, then where *was* she?

It was at that moment that my gaze fell on Rex's cage, and I saw Leia's tail disappearing inside it. *Oh, no!*

"Leia!" I shouted, desperately rushing forward. "Get away from there! Rex is in a bad mood!"

"Hi," I heard Leia chirp from inside the cage. "How are you? I'm Leia! I don't know if I've told you that yet. Ooh, you're looking a little low in spirits, Rex. Can I sing you a lullaby? Would you like me to get a big ol' hambugger for you? I hear there are some on my other friend Buster's head."

At that instant, I charged into the cage, paws flying royally across the floor, teeth bared and ready to rip into some Doberman should he try to hurt Leia in any way. Sure, he had showed signs of liking Leia. But when Rex was "a little low in spirits," as Leia put it, there was no telling what he might do. By the way, whenever Leia describes a dog as "a little low in spirits," that means the dog is standing up, hackles raised, fangs flashing, and lips curled. To put it simply, Leia's not good at interpreting canine body language, even though she's a canine herself.

As I mentioned, I went zooming into the cage. As I mentioned, I looked magnificent as I did it. As I prefer *not* to mention, I banged, queenly nose first, right into Leia's hind end. Leia jumped, and when she did, I fell flat on my schnauzer. *Egh! My dignity!*

"Oh! Hi, Mommy. Did you bring the big ol' hambugger from Buster's head?" Leia inquired, not seeming to notice the fact that I was lying with my face planted on the ground.

"*No,* Leia," I growled, standing up and shaking off. I glared at Rex who, as I had predicted, was in the attack position. "I have some questions for you, bozo."

Leia looked at the ceiling, shaking her head at me. "Oh, Mommy. I already asked him if he wanted a big ol' hambugger."

My eyelid twitched. Then, deciding to ignore Leia, I let out a breath and declared, "Listen, Rex, I demand that you—"

"Tear you to shreds?" Rex guessed, moving forward menacingly. "With pleasure."

"Ooh! Ooh! Me first!" Leia cried, hopping up and down in a circle. "Me first! Pick me! Pick me! Pick me!"

Ugh. Clearly Leia didn't understand the meaning of tearing someone to shreds.

Reaching over our heads, Rex caught the chain-link door with his paw and started to pull it closed, intending to trap us inside. "Leia. Go. *Now,*" I urged in a soft tone.

Obediently, Leia, with a merry wave to Rex, turned and hopped for the rapidly closing gap. She reached the opening and plunged into it, but unfortunately…

Okay, this was the most horrible time for me to have a faulty memory, but I had completely and utterly forgotten that Leia has…um…*problems* with tight spaces. BIG problems. *Why did I tell her to go first?*

Sure enough, I heard a squishing sound, and then a scrabbling of pawnails, and then a defeated squeak. “Mommy! I’m *stuck*!” wailed Leia in despair.

I’m stuck, too, I thought, staring up at Rex in horror. *Stuck with a bloodthirsty Doberman pinscher!*

“Leia! You fool!” I exploded as Rex grinned evilly, his paw still firmly holding the door three-fourths closed. Since I couldn’t get past Leia’s mass, I backed up as far as I could, my bottom pressing against the chain-link. I smiled innocently up at Rex. "Hello?" I tried.

"I told you that if you bothered me again, you'd be sorry," Rex reminded me unpleasantly.

"You know dogs don't have very good memories," I attempted, wagging my tail weakly. "Next time you need to send me a text message. Yeah, that's it! All reminders are done by text messages these days."

Rex tilted his head in confusion. "*What?*"

"Texting. Don't tell me you've *never* heard of texting!" I exclaimed, feigning astonishment. "Why, you're not a very modern Doberman, are you? Still hanging in times before the current cell phone? Well, never fear, my friend. I would be happy to update you on—"

"No," Rex snapped. "I don't care about a cell phone."

"Ah, then can I interest you in a discussion of an iPod?"

"No. You can interest me in *no* discussion at all."

"Good idea. I'll be quiet so you can text me," I chirped, hoping this was one dimwitted Doberman. He wasn't.

Rex moved forward, managing to maintain his hold on the cage door.

"Mommy!" yelped Leia. "Help!"

"Leia, *I'm* the one who needs help," I mumbled, trying to maintain my clueless grin. I turned my attention back to Rex, who was licking his lips in anticipation of making me into a Shih Tzu Sandwich. "So, do you need a cell phone?" I questioned shakily. "I mean, obviously, you're *not* texting me. You must not have a cell phone. That's no problem. There's an electronics store right by the shopping mall, and—"

"You can stop talking now, runt," snarled Rex. He opened his mouth and plunged toward me.

In order to do that, however, he had to loosen his grip on the cage, and Leia took that opportunity to pop out of the tight spot, pulling the cage door open unintentionally as she did so. Since his paw was still planted on the chain-link, he tumbled forward, his nose colliding with the door, and flew almost completely over my head. *Almost* completely.

"Rex," I gasped out, shoving at his chest with my queenly paws, "get *off*!"

Rex, shaking his head in surprise, took a moment to regain his bearings, then turned and looked down at me, showing his teeth. I, meanwhile, continued to push up on his ribcage with my dainty front paws to no avail. *Gee, for a thin little Doberman, Rex feels like he weighs as much as an elephant!*

"Oh, Mommy! Why is Rex on top of you?" Leia asked, plopping onto her bottom in the hall and scratching one floppy ear. "Are you playing Hide-and-Seek? He can feel you underneath him, Mommy. That's not a very good hiding place."

Growling, Rex kept his eyes riveted on me. In my present position ("p" words!), I was helpless and completely within reach of Rex's saliva-covered jaws. *Oh, no!*

Then, just as Rex was about to make me into a Shih Tzu Shish Kebab, a voice distracted us both. "Luna!" Creeper called from the top of the cages. "You'll never guess what I found!"

A split second later, the ghost of No-Slack Jack dropped on the floor—just beyond Leia.

CHAPTER SIXTEEN (XVI, *Dieciséis*)

A Shocking New Development

"WHAT?" I exclaimed in genuine shock.

Rex leapt up to examine Creeper's find, and I let out a long, relieved breath, then stood up myself and raced over to the ghost.

"Mommy, look!" Leia cried, grinning down at the mummified form. "It's Mr. Ghost! I wonder if he's feeling okay. He's just sitting there. Maybe I should feel his forehead."

Leia placed a paw to the ghost's *completely solid* "forehead," but before she could make a diagnosis, I stepped in and sniffed the ghost up and down. "Toilet paper!" I announced.

Rex, who had been sniffing the ghost's face, declared, "Flashlights and Christmas lights!"

Squinting, I turned to look at what Rex was referring to. Yes, flashlights appeared to have been fashioned to the so-called "ghost" to make convincing eyes. Red Christmas lights were glued into the mouth as teeth.

"Whoa. I wonder who his dentist is," Leia mused, bobbing her head back and forth to an imagined musical beat.

Seconds before I could inspect the ghost further, Creeper flew down from the top of the cages, landing right next to me. In triumph, he reached over and ripped some of the "cloth" from the ghost. "Toilet paper," he said, dropping it on the floor. "And look what's underneath."

Glow rods were taped to the surface of the supposed "ghost of No-Slack Jack," hidden by the toilet paper, but still able to give off an eerie light.

Proudly, Creeper then held up a long stick to which several strings had been fastened and connected to the ghost. "It's a puppet!"

I nodded. "Whoever was controlling the puppet was up there, on top of the cages. That's why whenever the ghost flew away, it flew onto the kennel tops." I turned. "Leia, when Rex let you up there, you saw all the spare toilet paper that the vile villains used to wrap up this ghost."

"But who did all this?" Rex demanded.

"Not to mention *why*," Creeper put in.

I thought long and hard while Creeper began peeling more toilet paper from the ghost's form. "I don't know," I finally admitted.

Just as Creeper was about to discover what the main body of the ghost was composed of, however, a horrendous shriek came from the other end of the hall.

"Luna!" shouted Benson, racing down the aisle toward us with his Beagle ears flying. He stopped just before us, taking a brief instant to stare at the marionette. But whatever he had to tell me appeared more important than his momentary shock, and he jerked his head up. "Luna, help! I can't find Darling anywhere!"

A stone dropped to the bottom of my stomach. "Darling is… *missing*?" This was an incredibly new and unexpected development.

Benson nodded, his eyes desperate. "You *have* to help! She's not in her cage! She's not in the hall! She's not *anywhere*! She wouldn't just disappear on her own!" He was panting so loudly that I sighed irritably, and he stopped.

"Listen, Benson, if we finish dissecting this supposed 'ghost,' then it might hold a clue as to the identity of the culprits behind this mystery," I pointed out.

"And if we know who is behind this mystery, we can arrest them and get Darling back," Creeper added reassuringly.

Benson began shaking. "But I'm just so worried about her!"

I waved my paw. "I have the perfect solution to your problem."

Benson looked hopeful. "Yes? What is it?"

"Forget about your problem," I advised, straightening. *Wow. I am awesome as both a detective and a psychologist.*

"What?" Benson asked, his tail sinking and his eyes growing considerably. "*Forget* about Darling?"

"No, no. Forget about *your problem.*"

"My problem is that Darling is missing."

"Very good. I'm glad you've gotten that off your chest. Now forget all about it."

"How can I?"

"That's easy. Just wait five minutes. I hear that's about as long as a dog's memory lasts," I answered helpfully. *Man, I'm good!* "By the way," I added with a snooty smile ("s" words!), "you owe me about twenty thousand pounds of kibble."

Benson's face twisted in confusion. "Why?"

"Because I've just provided you with a large and vital amount of psychological help!" I exploded. "Should I not be paid for such a service?"

Benson blinked. "So, are you going to help me find Darling or not?"

"*Yes,* we are," Creeper cut in before I could regally reply ("r" words!). He patted the semi-wrapped form of the fake ghost. "Just let us finish this so we can find out what's underneath all of this toilet paper."

"A cardboard roll?" Leia guessed.

"Leia, that is what's underneath *most* toilet paper," I allowed, and Leia's tail began to thump. "However"—Leia's expression sagged—"it is obvious that the crooked crooks behind this hoax wrapped some sort of *something* in toilet paper. So far, we have been unable to find out exactly what it is."

"Ooh! Ooh! I bet it's a cardboard roll!" Leia shouted, jumping up and down.

I huffed. The shape of the fake ghost was *obviously* not that of a cardboard roll. Oh, well—I would just let Leia have her idea. It's best not to argue with my silly sidekick.

While we spoke, Rex was busy tearing the toilet paper from the fake ghost's face. When his eyes fell on what was underneath, he jumped back with a surprised bark. That got all of our attention. Creeper, Leia, Benson, and I jerked around to stare.

"What is it?" quavered Benson, still clearly shaken from finding out that Darling was missing.

I grinned. "Just as I suspected."

"A fuzzy, dog-shaped cardboard roll!" Leia exclaimed, smiling. She wiggled happily. "I'm such a good guesser!"

Ugh. What awful alliteration ("a" words!).

"No, Leia," I corrected. "*Not* a fuzzy, dog-shaped cardboard roll—a gigantic, dog-shaped *stuffed animal.*"

"With cardboard taped to the sides for wings," Creeper put in. He turned to the fake ghost's back and ripped away more of the toilet paper.

Leia put on her Thinking Face. Then she scratched at a flea. "Oh." Suddenly, she looked up at the ceiling. "Hey, there are loudspeakers in here!"

My mind immediately began working. Leia's random comment might actually prove to be significant. *Loudspeakers? Could the ghost's voice have come over the loudspeakers?*

Creeper was apparently thinking on this, too, as he had one paw to his chin. However, Benson rudely interrupted my queenly contemplation at that moment.

"But why would anyone go through this whole elaborate scheme?" wailed the Beagle in despair. "Where would a shelter animal get all of this stuff, anyway?"

"They wouldn't," I told him bluntly. "The culprits of this mystery are, in fact, *not* shelter animals."

"That's right," Creeper agreed. "Whoever did the ghost's voice was in the security office, talking over the loudspeakers, when the guard wasn't there."

"So, what does this all mean?" demanded Benson.

I grinned. "It means that those loser Labs are behind Darling's dognapping!"

CHAPTER SEVENTEEN (XVII, *Diecisiete*)

Caught—Or So We Thought

Benson's jaw dropped. "What? How could that be? Those Labs are the nicest—"

"I don't want to hear it," I interrupted. "Those loser Labs are *not* nice, let alone the *nicest* anything! But anyway, we have to arrest them quickly so we can find Darling."

"But why would they dognap Darling?" Benson wanted to know.

I shook my head, clicking my tongue in disapproval of his lack of logic. "Benson, I suspect that perhaps Darling found out about their whole scheme, so they had to remove her from the picture."

This apparently didn't comfort Benson, for he hung his head and a tear dripped from one of his brown eyes onto the concrete floor. "I'll never see her again," he sniffled.

"Dog up," I urged him. "You're not a puppy anymore. You've graduated from soft food to hard kibble!"

Benson tilted his head, momentarily forgetting his predicament. "What does *that* have to do with anything?"

"Apparently you *haven't* graduated from direct speech to playing on words," I muttered in annoyance. Then I huffed and turned to Creeper. "All right, Creeps. I know that Spot is in the cage down there." I jerked my head in the cage's direction. "I can arrest him really quickly. Meanwhile, you and Benson can go apprehend Spike and Specks. Call for assistance if you need it."

"What do I do?" Leia wanted to know. She thumped her tail eagerly.

"You come with me," I told her. She smacked her lips and grinned, thumping her tail some more. *Well, at least she's happy about it.*

"What about me?" growled Rex.

Gulp. "Um, you can guard the side door in case one of them tries to escape to the outside," I squeaked weakly. He narrowed his eyes, but Creeper spoke before either of us could choose a further course of action.

"Wait a minute. I have an idea that can get the Labs here so we don't have to search them out," Creeper said decisively.

"Well, what is it?" I demanded impatiently. Normally, a queenly Shih Tzu detective like me retains an enormous amount of patience, but this situation called for immediate action, not calm discussions, so of course I…Never mind.

Creeper sat back on his haunches and shrieked dramatically, "OH, NO! IT'S THE GHOST OF NO-SLACK JACK! WHATEVER SHALL WE DO?"

Oh! I see! Creeper's acting like the ghost is appearing so all those loser Labs will hurry up and get here to find out what's up! Then we'll arrest them! Wow, Creeper is so smart. He takes after me.

Catching on, I immediately yapped, "OH, SOMEBODY HELP US! THE GHOST OF NO-SLACK JACK HAS ARRIVED! HELP! HELP! *HEEEEEEEEEEEEEEEEEEEEEEEEEELP*!"

Benson joined in our yammering, as did Rex, but Leia quickly glanced wildly about her, searching for the ghost. *Ugh!* Couldn't she tell we were faking? Oh, well. That's Leia for you.

Eventually, when her attention span for the ghost had reached its limit, Leia plopped onto her bottom, waved her paws, and sang, "*There are lots of snowflakes and ice down where the penguins roam. The continent, it's Antarctica, and that's the penguins' home*!"

As Leia plunged into the chorus, I jerked my head to the left, still shouting, as I realized Spike and Specks were hurtling right for the center of the hall. Spot had slipped out of his cage and was hurrying for us, too, and all were gazing around in bewilderment.

"What's wrong?" cried Spot, skidding to a stop near me.

"Where is the ghost?" added Spike, trying to hide his confusion.

I grinned as Rex and the rest of us stepped back, revealing the shredded-up "ghost" for all to see. "*Here's* your ghost," I declared proudly, puffing out my queenly chest. "And I do mean *your* ghost, as in *you're* the ones that built it. Isn't that right, Spot?"

"No, no!" Spot protested. "I don't know anything about this!"

Spike and Specks had paled, if that's possible for yellow and brown Labradors, and their eyes never left the fake ghost, even as Creeper and I began to explain (and Leia continued singing).

"You said your owner has a daughter named Emma with lots of toys," I announced proudly. "You simply used one of her life-sized stuffed animals for the ghost's basic shape, two of her flashlights for its bright eyes, Christmas lights for its teeth, and glow sticks to make the 'spirit' appear more believable. You controlled it like a puppet so it would look like it was flying. You also wrapped it with toilet paper to create a convincing ghoul, but not convincing enough to fool Luna, Puppy Detective!"

"No, no, that's not how it went—" Spike tried, but I instantly interrupted him. Yes, little Luna kid fans, interrupting is rude. But hey, the Bible says not to lie. Spike was about to lie. So I cut into his lie before he could complete it. Technically, I saved him from a serious sin ("s" words!). End of story.

"Plus," I snapped, "we found Spot's fur at the original scene of the crime."

"You did?" Spot asked, his eyes going wide.

"That's right, bonehead. I knew there was something fishy about you three from the very start," I declared royally, straightening. "So now you guys are going to jail."

"No way!" With that, Specks whirled and tried to race past Rex for the side door, but Rex executed a quick martial arts move and had Specks and Spike on their backs with their paws in the air quicker than you could say, "Simple Simon was a pie man." He loomed over both of them, his teeth bared, daring them to get up. They didn't.

"What I can't figure out is, why did you do all of this?" Creeper demanded.

"I didn't!" wailed Spot desperately.

I jabbed my paw at his nose. "*Yes*, you did, and you know it!"

"No!" Spot insisted. "I *didn't*! Honest!"

I jumped up, slapping him across the nose. I didn't want to hear it anymore. He was guilty, and that was the end of it. Then I turned to Spike and Specks. "Both of you, confess!" I ordered. "You created the hoax of No-Slack Jack!"

"Okay, okay," squeaked Spike quite girlishly as Rex glared down at him. "We did it. Just me and Specks, though, not Spot."

This made me give a little hop. By this time, Mocha, Buster, Cat-Eyes, and many other animals had gathered around, making escape almost impossible, even for Spot, who was closest to the side door. Most were trying to get a good look at the fake ghost, relieved that a restless and vengeful spirit really wasn't terrorizing the shelter.

"Wait a minute! Rewind," I ordered Spike. "Spot is *not* guilty?"

"No," Specks admitted carefully. "He's the only innocent one. We planted his fur at the crime scene to frame him."

"But *why* did you do all this?" Creeper repeated, showing slight signs (lots more "s" words—I'm good!) of annoyance. That surprised me. It took a lot to drive Creeper off the edge.

"And where's Darling?" yelped Benson, unable to contain himself any longer.

"And where's the big ol' hambugger?" Leia contributed, looking about ready to burst into tears.

Spike sighed. "Sorry, Benson. Darling's not here anymore."

"We promised that we would get her back to her owners, the Jensons, if she would help us control the ghost so *we* wouldn't be dogs of interest," Specks added.

"It's relatively easy to get up onto the top of the cages if you're a big dog," Spike put in.

"Yes, and she's big, just like us, so she was the perfect accomplice," Specks continued. He then muttered thoughtfully, "But before she agreed to control the ghost, she wanted to see if she could get up on the cages. Jamming some newspaper in the door so it wouldn't close all the way, she climbed up during the day, while the humans were out and most of the dogs were sleeping. When she saw that Leia was coming out of their cage, Darling hid until she had a chance to slip back into the enclosure unnoticed."

So that's why the door was open when Leia went to play Toss the Squeaky Toy with Rex!

"When Darling controlled the ghost and imitated its voice, it made both of us look innocent because we were standing right next to Luna when the ghost appeared. Afterward, we took her back to the Jenson house just like we promised," Spike explained, picking up the story for Specks.

I nodded. "That makes sense. She's only 'missing' now because she's back with her family."

"The big ol' hambugger left?" Leia asked, clearly alarmed.

I patted her shoulder. "There is no 'big ol' hambugger,' Leia."

Leia broke down sobbing. "BUT, MOMMY! YOU SAID THERE WAS A BIG OL' HAMBUGGER

ON BUSTER'S HEAD, AND HE SAID IT WAS A BOWLING BALL, AND NOW I'M ALL CONFUSED, MOMMY!"

Suddenly, Cat-Eyes marched up beside me, dropping onto her bottom and purring. "So I see you figured out who's behind the mystery."

"Hush up, cat. You're interfering with an interrogation." I suddenly stopped. "Wait a minute, Cat-Eyes. You might still be in on this whole crime. I suspect you because of that lie you told…Why did you beg to be let out of your cage when we first got here if you could already pop the latch yourself anyway?"

"You never figured it out," Cat-Eyes cooed with great pleasure. Creeper looked at her expectantly. Sighing, Cat-Eyes explained, "Well, you see, I wanted to be let out so bad. Those losers"—she gestured at Spike and Specks—"never let me out of my cage, and I didn't know how to get out on my own. I finally got fed up and decided to teach myself how to get out." Cat-Eyes flipped her tail. "So I focused extremely hard and finally twisted my arm at just the right angle in order to flip the latch. Make sense now?"

I blinked, nodded, then turned back to Spike and Specks as Leia started to sing, "*Yankee Doodle went to town, riding on a pony…*"

I ignored her as Creeper exploded, "For goodness' sake, can you street mutts please tell us why you did all this?"

Suddenly, Spike plunged his jaws upward and into Rex's throat. Yelping, Rex leapt backward, his back paw coming down on Benson's front paw. Benson yelped, too, and Spike and Specks, leaping to their feet, shoved through the crowd of animals and raced for the side door.

"Stop them!" I yapped as I hurried to push through the animals in pursuit. "Stop them, stop them, *stop them*!"

CHAPTER EIGHTEEN (XVIII, *Dieciocho*)

An Unlikely Meeting

As it turned out, the side door, inconveniently, wasn't even locked. Desperately, Spike and Specks threw themselves against the door, Spike's paw came down on the handle, and within the next few seconds, they were racing across the dark parking lot.

Slightly lit by the rising sun in the distance, the parking lot was nevertheless intimidating. But nothing is too intimidating for Luna, Puppy Detective, and before the door could close, Creeper and I were hot on their tails, along with Rex and Spot. Unfortunately, the door swung shut just as Leia wriggled out. The other shelter animals flocked toward the door, but they didn't make it out in time, and as I continued my pursuit, I could hear them howling. A few began slamming on the door, but none seemed to realize that, in order to get out, they had to twist the handle first. *Egh.* Sometimes I wonder if I'm the only intelligent dog on this planet.

"Wait up, Mommy!" Leia pleaded, racing along on her tubby legs.

"Stop, villains!" I shouted as Spike and Specks neared the sidewalk.

Then something strange happened.

The American Staffordshire Terrier—the one I met before being locked up in the shelter—leapt out in the crooked canines' path, blocking their escape. His two Mini Bull Terrier friends took up his flank, baring their teeth. The white one let a long line ("l" words!) of drool dribble ("d" words—gee, I can't make it look too easy, can I?) onto the sidewalk.

"Halt!" shouted the American Staffordshire Terrier, who I recalled was known as Jake.

"Oh, look, Mommy! It's our pit bull friend!" screeched Leia quite unhelpfully.

Surprisingly, Spike and Specks skidded to quick stops, ending up almost nose-to-nose with Jake, their eyes wide. "No-Slack Jack?!" they cried out in unison.

That was about the time Creeper, Rex, Spot, and I arrived on the scene. Huffing and puffing (I'm not used to exercising on my cases—but I'm *not* fat), I glared from Jake to Spike and Specks, from

Jake to Spike and Specks, and back to Jake. "Who are you, and what do you have to do with all this?" I demanded, baring my royal teeth and arching my queenly back. Creeper arched his back, too, and let out a caterwaul.

"You're a-alive?" stammered Spike, addressing the pit bull.

"We thought you were d-dead," added Specks.

"Well, as you can see, I am *not* dead," Jake replied. He rolled his eyes. "Spike, Specks, what sort of ruckus have you caused?"

"It wasn't our fault!" wailed Spike. "We were just trying to help your image! We knew Spot wouldn't go along with it because he is always so honest and pure-hearted. We *had* to frame him, see, and had we known you were alive, we would've—"

"Back up!" I yipped, jumping between Spike and Jake and waving my paws. "WHAT IS GOING ON HERE?"

"Yeah, I wanted to know that, too," spoke up the brown-and-white Mini Bull Terrier.

"Me, too, Jake," drooled the white one.

"Me, too!" chirped Leia. She scratched at a flea. "Wait, are we talking about the big ol' hambugger or the penguins in Antarctica?"

Jake sighed, ignoring Leia, his eyes fixed on a trembling Spike and Specks. "I'd like to know that, too," he growled, gazing intently at them. "So, tell me, boys. What have you been up to?"

"Well," Specks began solemnly, glancing down at me, "this is Luna, Puppy Something-or-Other, and Luna, this is the dog that was formerly known as No-Slack Jack. His name has always really been Jake, but he was such a feared street dog that everybody nicknamed him No-Slack Jack. We were part of his gang—Spike, Spot, and me. Then he was taken to the shelter, and word got to us that he was pummeled by a dog called Rex."

At this point, Rex curled his lip and snarled something under his breath. I didn't catch what he said, and I was sure glad of that because Rex isn't in the habit of making pleasant comments, let's just say.

"That forced No-Slack Jack to leave the shelter and lie low," Specks continued. "He was humiliated, having finally been beaten by another animal. News like that doesn't stay quiet, and soon everyone started talking about how No-Slack Jack was really a big wimp."

What? Did he just call me "Luna, Puppy Something-or-Other"? What a bozo!

"After he left Sierra Sunrise, word on the street was that he died," Spike jumped in. "His gang gave up on him and went their separate ways because they had no leader. Naturally, my brothers and I stayed together and eventually found a home with the shelter's security guard. When Specks and I realized that Rex was at the shelter we were protecting, we decided to create the hoax of No-Slack Jack. We wanted to bring the great street dog's name back to the top of the Dogs to Fear list."

At that point, I interrupted. "Am I on that list?" I wanted to know.

Spike shook his head. "It's a metaphor. But no."

"We're really sorry, Jake," Specks muttered. "We didn't know you were still alive."

"Boys, after my humiliation at the shelter"—Jake cast a glance at Rex, who growled, but Jake just looked back at Spike and Specks—"I decided the life of a street fighter was just too pointless. So, I resolved to completely change my ways."

Leia clapped her paws. "Yay!"

Jake, unable to resist Leia's cute, clueless expression, patted my goofy daughter on the head before concluding, "I went into the sheriff business, and now I help street dogs turn their lives around, too.

Anyway, these are my two deputies, Mug and Spiffy, who are reformed street dogs themselves."

"That's right," the white one, Spiffy, drawled.

"Well, Jake, we're sorry that we terrorized this whole shelter," Spike mumbled, staring at the ground. "We were just trying to help win back your tough reputation. That's all. Oh, and we wanted to make Rex miserable too, so sorry, Rex, about the pins."

Rex growled in response.

"Boys, I understand your intentions were of the loyalist origin," Jake began, "however, I must point out that the actions resulting from your thoughts were wrong."

Spike and Specks let out breaths of apology.

"But there is hope for you yet!"

Spike and Specks jerked their eyes back to Jake. "Really?" they both cried in unison.

"Yes!" Jake encouraged. "You, along with Spot"—Spot smiled and wagged his tail slowly—"could become part of my deputy force."

"You mean it?" squealed Specks in delight.

"Yay!" repeated Leia, clapping her paws again.

"Yes, I mean it," Jake confirmed with a smile. "That same intelligence that allowed you to build something bad can be used to build something good. What do you say?"

All three Labradors leapt onto Jake and started licking him across the face. He took it for a little while, laughing and swatting them playfully, but then he grew serious and shoved them off. Clearly he still retained a strong sense of dignity that included no hugging.

"And the first thing we'll do," Spike resolved, "is drop by Darling's house and have a little talk with her."

Jake grinned. "You can explain to me who this 'Darling' dog is on the way. But before we do that..." Jake turned and looked down at me. "How about we take you home, little doggy?"

I jumped. "How did you know I was owned?"

He looked me up and down. "You're too snooty for a street dog," he said simply.

I grinned and puffed out my chest. "Let's go back and explain to the shelter animals all that has happened. Then we can dispose of the fake ghost and be on our way."

"So I guess you're not so bad anymore," Rex told Jake with a small smile. "I mean, when you were at the shelter, you were *sooo* annoying with all of your tough talk. But…now…Maybe we can be friends."

Jake smiled back. "That would be nice."

I was hardly listening. *Home. Home! We are going home! Home to Emily and my Snuggy Rug and treats and squeaky toys and a game of Canine Checkers! Home to Pip, who definitely needs punishment! And most important of all—home to happy endings!*

EPILOGUE

After we finally got the ghost mess cleaned up at the shelter, we had to skedaddle really quickly because it was almost opening time. Spike, Spot, and Specks left with their owner, promising to later help Jake reform Darling.

But above all, Creeper, Leia, and I arrived home that very day, glowing with the pride of having just solved another mystery. We immediately tunneled under the gate and into our yard, where Emily discovered us. To teach Pip a lesson, we scared the annoying Siamese off the fence about twenty times that afternoon. Then we squished Lily's tail and barked Monikk into next week. When evening came, we settled down to a quiet game of Canine Checkers (at least it was quiet until Leia started singing the "Penguin Song").

Occasionally, Jake dropped by, updating us on all of our shelter friends (and enemies). A family in Hereford, near Sierra Vista, adopted Mocha and Benson; Cat-Eyes went to a little old lady who already owns a bunch of cats, and Buster ended up living with a woman who constantly bathes him. Jake lent a paw to Rex by finding him a home across the street from the Doberman that Leia has a crush on. And Spike, Spot, and Specks are still working with the former No-Slack Jack to help street dogs turn their lives around.

In short, it was a successfully concluded mystery, solved by a very capable Shih Tzu detective, otherwise known as *me.* Basically, all I have to say now regarding the intrigue of the ghost of No-Slack Jack is one thing:

Case closed.

The End

The contents of this book have been read and approved by:

Luna Bella Hickman

Leia Jewel Hickman

ABOUT THE AUTHOR

Kesmine Grace Hickman, a thirteen-year-old girl who lives in Sierra Vista, Arizona, has always possessed an unusual passion for creating thrilling and adventurous mystery stories. This talent allowed her to publish a book when she was only ten, called *Kathy Carts.* At age twelve, Kesmine decided to conjure up a new protagonist for the plot of another mystery series. The character, based on Kesmine's charismatic Shih Tzu, Luna, is a shockingly snooty super sleuth that makes her first appearance in *Luna: Puppy Detective #1: Catnapped!* This death-defying dog continues her venturing in *Luna: Puppy Detective #2: No-Slack Jack,* as well as the entire *Luna: Puppy Detective* series, which Kesmine is currently working on. Aside from writing, Kesmine enjoys Taekwondo, soccer, horseback riding, spending time with her family, and playing with her four Shih Tzu dogs: Luna, Luke, Leia, and Leopold.

Made in the USA
San Bernardino, CA
18 October 2013